A SOLID CORNERSTONE

THE BUILDERS, BOOK 5

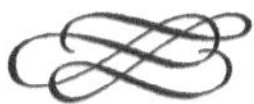

VANESSA GRAY BARTAL

DRY CREEK PRESS

CHAPTER 1

They thought he was a gangster. That was the first thing Joseph Samperi realized on his first day in his new school, in his new town, in his new state of Kentucky. In retrospect, he shouldn't have worn the black t-shirt. It didn't help that he was large for his age, much larger and more muscular than all the other seventh graders.

"Are y'all, like, in a gang?" That had been the first question a boy posed to Joe as soon as he saw him sitting quietly at a desk in his classroom. The boy's accent was molasses thick with a twang that made it hard to discern his words. For Joe, who had only left Brooklyn three days ago, the contrast was so jarring it felt like being in another country. He was used to traffic, cement, and the hustle and bustle of the city. Here there was rolling pastureland and horses, everywhere horses. The closest Joe had ever been to a horse was in Central Park, and even then they had scared him.

He must have been glowering at the kid as he tried to understand his words and their meaning because, after a few beats, the kid scurried away as if afraid Joe might produce a tire iron and brain him. In his current mood, he might. He hated being the new kid, hated being in a strange place away from his friends and family. His parents had never so much as taken a vacation. For them, going into Manhattan once a year had been an exotic adventure. And now all of a sudden they were the type of people to move halfway across the country and resettle in rural Kentucky. Worse, they were living in a barn. What would kids make of that when they got hold of it? Would they think Joe and his family were poor? *Were* they poor? In Brooklyn, they had been like everybody else. Here they were painfully different.

Being uprooted and yanked away from everything familiar had led Joe to a few uncomfortable realizations about himself. First, he was shy. Second, he was a coward. Back home he'd had a large group of friends and, together, they had been daring and unstoppable. With them at his side, he could do anything and practically had. True, he had done a few things he wasn't proud of, like boosting a few hubcaps and hood ornaments, but most of that had been about proving himself and not a desire to steal or make money off of what they stole. But here, in the middle of nowhere, he had zero desire to meet new people or explore. Worse, those were the two things his parents wanted him to do the most.

"Go out, meet the neighbors, hang out by that creek. Turn over rocks, fish, look for animals." They had said those words to him repeatedly since the move. Joe would rather fall down an elevator shaft than make the long trek next door and introduce himself. And he had no idea what to do with a creek or how to fish or what to expect if he ever got around to turning over any rocks. Lucky for him, he was always needed as a babysitter for his four younger siblings.

"I can't leave them alone," he had told his parents, pointing to the wild bunch running in a circle around the middle of the barn.

"Take them with you," his father, who was busy trying to renovate the barn, had sounded almost desperate for quiet. So Joe had shepherded the kids outside and anxiously watched over them like a mother hen while they ran pell-mell around their new acreage. It had been easier to watch them in the city, where parks were nice and enclosed. All this freedom was stifling. And then school began and life became even worse.

A girl sat in front of him, her long blond hair dangling to the middle of her back. Joe sat up a little straighter, though he didn't know why. Back home he had barely started to notice girls. At the beginning of the summer, he had kissed Angelina Delbecchio behind the Gray's Papaya. He had done it on a dare but found it much pleasanter than expected. This girl was loads prettier than Angelina.

She turned and gave him a soft and gentle smile and something in Joe's heart went *ping!* "Hey," she said.

"Hi," was the best he could manage, and it came out in a croak.

"Psst." The boy who had asked him a question earlier was now trying to get his attention. "Don't talk to her."

"Why not?" Joe whispered.

"Because she and her family are trash," the boy said. He whispered the words, but they carried. The girl in front of Joe had turned back around, but she had tucked her hair behind her ear, leaving it visible. The tip turned bright pink. His heart began to hammer hard, and his fists were curled. He found that he wanted to hit the boy, to smash his fist into his face and pop his nose until it bled. How could he say something so mean about a girl whose only crime was to say hello to the new kid?

The teacher arrived, class began, and a crisis was averted.

Lunch arrived and Joe's dread increased. Where would he sit? To his relief, kids were allowed to sit outside, as long as the weather was nice. He took his bagged lunch—stuffed to the hilt with his mother's homemade goodies—and went in search of a refuge. The upside to having a lot of land nearby was that it was easy to find a spot to be alone. Joe scanned the expanse of the playground and saw at least a dozen places he could sit and eat in peace. Then he saw the blond girl from earlier sitting by herself beneath a tree. Her name was Sydney, he learned as soon as class began. Before he could talk himself out of it, he walked toward her and sat down.

She looked up in surprise. "You shouldn't sit by me," she warned.

"You want me to go?" he asked, hoping he didn't sound as hurt as he felt. The contact with her marked the first time he had ever reached out to anyone.

"No," she said hastily. "But other kids won't like it."

He sat down and began unloading his lunch. "Why not?"

"It's hard to explain unless you've lived here a long time. People don't like my family."

"Why not?" Joe asked.

"Because they steal stuff and cause a lot of trouble," she said.

"Do you steal things?" Joe asked.

"No, not anymore. I did when I was little." She paused and looked down before continuing. "My parents made me because I could get away with it."

"Why'd you stop?" he asked.

Relieved he hadn't condemned her, she continued. "Because an old lady who lives in my neighborhood told me to."

"Just like that?" he said.

"She said it nice. If she had been mean about it, I probably would have kept doing it. But she's this sweet woman who has always given me candy or cookies. One day she took me aside and told me stealing was wrong and I shouldn't do it, not even for my parents. I know this is dumb, but before then, I didn't know it was wrong. It was how we grew up."

Joe tried to imagine his parents telling him to steal. When he was caught stealing a hubcap, his mother had spanked him with a spoon, despite the fact that she was barely taller than he was at the time. He had known it was wrong; he had known it even more after a spanking that did more to wound his pride than his backside. "What kind of tree is this?" he asked, glancing up at the gnarled old behemoth.

"A peach tree. It's super old. See the peaches?" She pointed to the little knobs of fuzzy peaches. There was a note of question in her tone, as if she couldn't believe he had no idea what sort of tree it was.

"I've never seen one." There were trees in the city, but none that bore fruit. "I've never had a peach before."

She stood and dusted her hands on her pants. He watched, fascinated, as she shucked off her shoes and shimmied up the tree. A minute later she returned with a shirtfront full of peaches. She set them on the ground, sorted through until she found the best one, and held it out to him.

Joe took a bite and, for the first time since the move, felt like life might one day be all right again. Sweet juice dribbled down his chin. He used the back of his hand to wipe it off. "I'm going to call you Peaches from now on," he declared.

Sydney gave him the smile that did the thing to his heart again. She tilted her head and leaned slightly closer. "What should I call you?"

He picked up a peach and tossed it in the air like a baseball, catching it without really looking. "I'm sure you'll come up with something eventually."

CHAPTER 2

He was awake. Sydney could hear him stirring. His alarm hadn't beeped yet, but sometimes he rose a few minutes early. The evidence needed to be destroyed, and quickly, but she couldn't resist one more glance at the test. *Negative.* How could it be negative? She was four days late. All the symptoms were there. She would test later in the day, to be sure. Sometimes the hormones took a while to appear. That was what all the websites said.

His feet hit the floor. Quickly, she wrapped the test in toilet paper and buried it in the middle of the trashcan. On top, it would be glaringly obvious, but on the bottom he might see it when he dumped the trash out. She knew what to do; this wasn't her first time on the rollercoaster. In fact, she had been on this particular ride far too long.

She washed her hands and reached for the towel as Joe opened the door. "You sick, Peaches?"

"No, a potty break."

"You've been having a lot of those lately," Joe said.

She was surprised he had noticed, he was such a heavy sleeper.

"I'll be late tonight. Big project," Joe said.

"I remember. You've had a lot of late nights lately."

"You know how it goes," he said.

She did, all too well. If she didn't trust him so much, she might be suspicious. As it was, she was learning indifference could be as painful as infidelity. "You want me to save supper?"

"I'm sure Ma will send something."

Good ol' Mama, she thought. Her mother-in-law, Marie Samperi, was well known for her authentic Italian cuisine. Sydney would never measure up. Somewhere along the way she had stopped trying.

"What have you got on tap today?" he asked.

"Lots of stuff," she hedged. For instance, she might try to watch an entire season of *Gilmore Girls* before he returned home.

"I'll try to call, if I get a minute, but you know how it is," he said.

She did. As a builder, summer was his busiest season. As a teacher, it was her break. They used to joke about their opposing schedules. When had that stopped?

"You going back to bed? It's early for you," he said.

There was a time when he would have been thrilled to see her up so early. He would have kissed her, hoping for more, and he wouldn't have had to hope too hard. Now she shuffled back to bed without so much as a peck goodbye.

She snuggled into bed and stared at the ceiling, listening to the familiar sounds of her husband getting ready. First he would shower, then he would shave. Once downstairs, the dim kitchen noises would filter up. Eventually the garage door opened and closed. He was gone. Sydney slipped out of bed and back to the bathroom. Picking through the trash with wrinkled nose, she plucked out the test and unwrapped it. Was that a line? She squinted and held it up to the light. No, no line.

She used the bathroom again, and the need for another test evaporated. There would be no baby this month, as there had been no baby for the last twelve years she had been trying.

Sydney washed her hands, went back to bed, pulled the blankets over her head, and cried.

The day was supposed to be a scorcher. Joe wasn't glad about that, but he was thankful for the heavy workload that would keep him busy from before sunup to after sundown.

His youngest brother, Moss, was waiting on him when he arrived, looking oddly serious and morose. "What's up?" Joe asked.

"Molly had to have an IV yesterday."

Joe set down his bag with a thump. "Aw, man. How's she doing?"

"Not great. Bella's teething and not sleeping well. Molly can't keep weight on. The day before the IV she threw up twenty times. I know because I counted."

Worry always looked wrong on Moss's face. He was a happy-go-lucky kid, always had been. And he'd been so ecstatically happy when his wife became pregnant shortly after their marriage. But then she developed hyperemesis gravidarum, extreme morning sickness. Molly was also their company's secretary, coolly efficient but also warm and friendly. She kept them all functioning like a well-oiled machine. Seemingly the only thing she couldn't do well was be pregnant.

"Is there anything we can do to help?" Joe asked. After initially avoiding Moss's first baby, Bella, for as long as possible, he and Peaches had now warmed to her and adored her. In fact, she spent the week with them while Moss and Molly took their honeymoon.

"Ma's with Bella today, but I'm sure she'll make the rounds soon. If Peaches could take a day with her, I'd appreciate it."

"Of course," Joe agreed.

Moss took a breath as if gearing himself up. "Also, I want Molly to take a few weeks off work. She might be sick the whole pregnancy, but it's supposed to get a little better after the first trimester."

Joe was torn between concern for Molly and concern for the company. Molly won. "Absolutely. How does she feel about that?"

For the first time, Moss grinned. "How do you think? But I'm not giving her a choice in the matter."

Joe grasped his shoulder and gave it a squeeze. Moss looked so desperately lovestruck and worried. Joe remembered when he used to feel that way, a frantic sort of ache, imagining the possibilities of what could happen to Peaches on his watch. But along the way there had been so much accumulated worry and upset it had settled down to a dull ache, a sort of background noise. Moss could take proactive steps to help Molly. There was nothing Joe could do for Peaches. He should know; he'd tried everything.

He shouldered his bag again, believing the day's biggest crisis had been dealt with, but his remaining siblings were queuing up to speak to him. Impossibly, the day's bad news had only begun.

CHAPTER 3

Everything was different in Kentucky. Joe's first birthday party in the state proved it. Back in Brooklyn they celebrated their birthdays with their family. His mother would invite the cousins and fry enough cannoli for an army. But here in Kentucky it was an all out event, or at least it was for Savannah Morgan's thirteenth birthday. Her family lived on one of the big horse farms at the edge of town and balloons lined the driveway, along with signs and banners.

"Must have cost a fortune," his mother murmured, sounding impressed and possibly a little intimidated. His mother had insisted on driving him and Peaches to the party, to make certain everything was on the up and up and no "hanky panky" would take place during his first boy/girl party. Joe thought if he was likely to commit hanky panky with anyone, it would be the girl in the back seat, but he didn't say so to his mother and risk not being allowed to go to the party. He'd been forced to ask a month ahead of time and wait patiently for his parents to come to a decision over whether or not he'd be allowed to go. Peaches hadn't even told her parents she was leaving the house for the night.

"The Morgans like to make it appear they're rich, but they're actually not," Peaches said. Joe darted a glance at her in the mirror, wondering over the slight bitterness in her tone. She was always so sweet. He wondered what had her riled tonight, but of course couldn't ask with his mother sitting there, eavesdropping on every word.

"Hmm," his mother said, repressing a smile as if she was in on some joke about the Morgans he didn't know. More often than not lately he had the oddest sensation that his mother and Peaches were on the same side, the one opposite from him. He wasn't certain if he should be heartened by that or chagrined. Of course he wanted his mom to like his best friend, but she was *his* best friend, not his mom's. It occurred to him he should probably be jealous of his mom's attention going to Peaches and not the other way around and stared out the window, confused and perplexed.

They finally reached the house at the end of the long lane and saw it lit up with thousands of white lights. Music blared from nearby and a dance floor had been erected.

Peaches gasped. "Dancing." She caught sight of Joe watching her and glanced away, blushing. "That's fancy."

Joe looked away, suddenly sad. Her thirteenth birthday was next month. He wondered if her parents would even remember. They didn't deserve her, that was for certain. He made a mental note to tell his mother to make a big fuss over her. His mom was really good at stuff like that, at making people feel special on their special days. Peaches needed more of that in her life, all of it she could get. He suddenly wanted to reach out and touch her and crossed his arms, flustered and confused. They were friends, best friends, had never tried to be anything more. But. *I can't stop thinking about her,* he thought, darting her a glance. She was staring at him. They quickly broke off eye contact and glanced away.

His mother led them onto the porch and rang the bell. Joe and Peaches stood behind her, suddenly feeling young and awkward. He wished they had never come. Neither of them liked their schoolmates, preferring instead the sole company of each other. Joe was shy and slow to warm up, hadn't done much more than nod hello at people all the months he'd been in school. Sydney was an outsider for different reasons, too often at the mercy of their teasing. Joe hovered protectively at school, offering a handy shield with his oversized body. But here with no teachers around to oversee them, what if he couldn't keep her safe from their harsh words?

He must have been scowling hard because Peaches stepped close and whispered in his ear. "It's going to be all right."

He let out the breath he didn't know he'd been holding and bent to whisper in her ear. "We're sticking together like glue. Don't let anyone split us up. Deal?" He held out his hand for her to shake. She nodded and placed her little palm in his, giving his hand a squeeze. He wanted to hold onto her hand, but his mom and Mrs. Morgan were there and seemed to be finishing their conversation. He let her hand go, clenching his fist, trying to hold on to the tingles her touch caused before they could disappear.

"Well, it looks like everything is in order," his mother said, turning her beaming smile on them. "Have fun, you two. I'll be back in a couple of hours." She hugged Joe and whispered in his ear. "No hanky panky."

Joe didn't reply, but his face blushed crimson. He could only hope Mrs. Morgan and Peaches hadn't overheard. Then his mother hugged Peaches and Joe had a new worry.

"Did my mom say anything to you?" he asked when his mother finally left and Mrs. Morgan directed them to the side of the house where everyone was waiting.

"Like what?" Peaches asked, looking up at him with a curious smile.

"Nothing, never mind." He swiped his hand over the back of his neck and sideswiped a pile of horse manure, barely avoiding it as he made a last minute leap. "I'm definitely not in Brooklyn anymore."

"How do you say happy birthday in Italian?" she asked.

"Technically you say *buon compleanno,* that's literally good birthday. But usually we say *taunti auguri,* best wishes."

She linked her arm with his and rested her head on his shoulder a minute. "I love that, love that you can speak a whole other language. You're so interesting, Joey."

Interesting? Him? "I'm not, though. I'm the most boring person I know."

"Are you joking? You can actually make things, something from nothing, like a magician."

"That's just pounding nails," he said, cheeks flushed with pleasure.

"Well, I think it's amazing. I think…" she broke off, glancing away.

He gave her arm a squeeze. "What?"

"Nothing. Oh, here we are." Suddenly they arrived, spilling into the twinkling fairy lights like a plane landing on a runway. Joe squinted, letting his eyes adjust, and found everyone staring at them. Belatedly he realized their arms were still linked. People had been asking them all year if they were boyfriend and girlfriend. They always answered the same, *We're just friends.* But they'd also never touched in front of anyone before, and rarely in private. And now here they were standing close, arms entwined in front of the entire seventh grade. He expected Peaches, who was private and couldn't stand to have anyone looking at her, to drop her arm and move away. Instead she moved closer, touching her head to his shoulder briefly again. It was a sweetly affectionate gesture, and if he didn't know better might have felt possessive.

"You made it." Savannah Morgan hurried over, skidding to a halt in front of Joe.

"Happy birthday, Savannah."

"Thanks, Joe," Savannah said, beaming.

"Happy birthday. Thank you for inviting us," Sydney added. Savannah's smile dimmed, her eyes bouncing between their linked arms with a little furrow between her brows. "It's so pretty here. I love the lights."

"Thank you," Savannah replied, but it sounded stiff and forced. "We're going to play some games soon. Maybe you'll be on my team." There was no mistaking the fact that she spoke only to Joe that time, but again Sydney was the one who answered.

"Sounds fun, we'll see." The two girls stared at each other, saying things with their eyes Joe didn't understand. All he knew was that he now sensed danger and gave Peaches' hand a little pat where it rested on his arm. Savannah noted the touch and whirled, ponytail swishing.

"What was that about?" Joe whispered.

"No idea," Peaches replied, staring up at him, green eyes wide and innocent. He loved her eyes, could probably stare at them for hours. He realized he was doing so now and ripped his attention away.

"What do you think she meant by games?" he asked.

"Probably spin the bottle."

His heart kicked. Angelina Delbecchio remained his lone kiss. He hoped he wouldn't have to have a repeat in front of all his classmates, as if he had any idea what he was doing. "Oh, man, you think?"

Peaches shrugged. "If so, make sure we're across from each other. Better chances of getting each other that way."

His gaze swung to her, but she was staring straight ahead, surveying everything. That almost sounded like…did she want to kiss him, want him to kiss her? Or was she merely trying to save him the misery and embarrassment of having to kiss one of their classmates? For that matter, he didn't want any of them kissing her. Already Cassius Carter was eyeballing her from across the way. Joe scowled at him and he turned away, caught and guilty. Sydney had no idea the way boys looked at her. Maybe there was a time long ago when they wanted nothing to do with her, and there were still a few mean kids, but heads turned where she went, shoulders straightened. She was the most beautiful girl he'd ever seen, possibly in the whole world, and the fact that she didn't realize was a puzzling mystery to him. *Maybe I should tell her.* The thought popped into his head unbidden, and he banished it. Boys didn't say things like that to girls, did they? Though he had told Peaches lots of things he'd never told anyone else, all his embarrassing secrets…

He leaned closer, whispering. "Peaches."

Her glance darted up to his, so open, so trusting. So pretty, so, so pretty.

"Um, you, um, you look, um, I think…" *You're bombing, reel it in.* "Want to get some punch?" His voice cracked, deepening his misery and horror. Cassius Carter took a step closer, as if he sensed Joe's misstep and was about to swoop in for the kill. Joe shot him a glare and he turned last minute, diverting to Sherry instead.

"Joe, is something wrong? Do you want to go? We can call your mom," she offered, face puckering in concern.

"No, why? Why do you think something is wrong?" Did she know how badly he was messing this up? Was it that obvious?

She picked up the hem of his t-shirt, twisting her fingers in it. "I know you don't like to be with people from school you don't know."

He picked up a chunk of her long hair, twisting his fingers in it the same way. "I know you don't like to be with people from school you do know." She laughed and it was like the sun breaking free of the clouds, all warm and beaming. It made him brave enough to continue. "Besides, I'm not with them. I'm with you. As far as I'm concerned, they don't even exist right now."

"Even Savannah?" she said.

He frowned, confused again by her curt tone. "Well, I mean it's her birthday, but otherwise I couldn't care less. Do you not like Savannah? I thought you two got along."

"We used to," Peaches said.

"What happened?" he asked. Had they fought and he missed it?

"This really cute boy from Brooklyn showed up and got between us." Her other hand joined its mate, both of them now twining in the soft material of his shirt.

"I really hope you're talking about me," he blurted.

She smiled up at him, cheeks flushing the prettiest shade of light pink he had ever seen. He stared at her, rapt. "There's no one else, Joey. No one else on earth."

He shifted slightly, using his body to block them from everyone else. "Peaches, I..."

"Game time," Savannah's mother loudly announced. "Everyone ready for some games?"

"It's a Morgan family conspiracy," Peaches muttered. Joe barked a laugh and pressed his hand to his mouth.

He thought she was joking, at least until Mrs. Morgan assigned them to teams and paired Joe with Savannah and Peaches with

Cassius. They played racing wheelbarrows, with the boys holding the girls by the ankles while they collected little plastic balls and tossed them into a basket. Joe was at least a foot taller than every other guy in attendance, with broad shoulders and developed muscles. He and Savannah should have been a lock on winning, except she kept collapsing in bursts of giggles. Unlike Peaches who moved with unwavering precision, picking up each ball in a grid-like pattern, Cassius's voice urging her on acting like nails on a chalkboard to Joe's already overblown jealousy.

When they won, it was almost more than he could stand. And when Peaches stood and high fived Cassius, Joe felt like his face might explode, as if all the pent up anger and frustration might shoot out of him like laser beams. Fists curled, he stood at the edge of the party while Savannah tittered, giggling over their loss. Man, girls were stupid about boys sometimes. Did they not realize winning was everything?

"Hard loss, Joseph," Peaches said from his other side. He might have thought she was poking at him, except he knew her so well now he could tell she wasn't.

"We would have won by even more. We would have won every point," he couldn't help but add.

"Then maybe it's better we didn't get paired together. World domination at someone else's birthday party might be too much," Peaches said.

Now Joe was grinning. No one but his family could make him turn a thundercloud into a smile. His family and Peaches.

Music started. After a few awkward attempts at eye contact and conversation, a few kids shuffled out onto the makeshift dance floor.

"Dancing," Peaches said softly, shooting a not-so-subtle glance in his direction. "Do you like dancing, Joey? You've never said."

He shook his head, fingers twining miserably together. He was so much taller than everyone else. Dancing made him feel conspicuous, as if he were Frankenstein stumbling around for everyone's inspection. *Look at the giant, uncoordinated freak.*

"Oh," Peaches said, clearly disappointed. Cassius Carter sidled closer. Joe reached for Peaches' hand and gave it a tug.

"But maybe it will be different with you," he said. It had to be. Everything else was. Dimpling in delight, she allowed him to lead her to the floor. He settled his arms around her waist, she pressed her palms to his chest. They started to sway awkwardly. Their height didn't line up. He was still painfully uncoordinated, more so compared to her easy grace. But he was right, too, because he suddenly didn't care. It was enough that he was finally holding Sydney Parker in his arms, and for the first time in his life he never wanted the music to end.

CHAPTER 4

The downstairs door opened and closed. Sydney didn't stir from beneath her blanket fort. The sounds now filtering up were as familiar to her as Joe's readiness routine. It was only a matter of time until they shifted upstairs. Maybe she dozed again. She couldn't be certain. She was certain she was now awake when the covers were ripped away from her face.

"I should wash the sheets, I think. Don't you think?" Her mother-in-law peered down at her, a look on her face Sydney knew well. It was a combination of love, concern, and consternation. It was a safe bet to say Marie Samperi had never lingered in bed her entire life, never buried herself beneath a mound of covers while the world passed her by, never hidden from her problems or wallowed in a depression so deep the light didn't penetrate anymore.

"They're probably fine," Sydney muttered, trying not to project her morning breath in Marie's direction.

"I should change them. I can work around you."

Translation: get up, you ridiculously lazy sloth.

"I'll help," Sydney said because it was what she should say and certainly not because she wanted to. She rolled out of bed, stumbling, blinking at the harsh light now filtering through the window. She had closed the blackout curtains, of course, but Mama Samperi had thrown them wide open. Sydney intended to help her mother-in-law peel the sheets off her bed and replace them with clean ones, but instead she got caught up staring at the world outside the window. Outside the world went on functioning as always, passing Sydney by. She should be out there. She should *want* to be out there. The problem was that she didn't want to want to. She had no energy even for recrimination for her sorry state. She had no energy to feel anything anymore. She was numb now, too numb to feel shame while her husband's mother cleaned her house and did her laundry. Too numb to be embarrassed over staring helplessly outside the window like an invalid in her pajamas while Marie, perfectly made up, cleaned the detritus of her life.

"There," Marie said, giving the clean sheets a smoothing pat.

Sydney went back to the bed and lay down. Marie perched on the edge of the bed and smoothed her hand over Sydney's hair, pushing it out of her face. Sydney closed her eyes, leaning in to the touch. It was a safe bet her own mother had never touched her that way. She yawned, shuddering, overwhelmed by the feelings that tried to intrude. With effort, she pushed them away. Numbness was so much easier than feeling, so much better than pain.

"Maybe you could talk to someone," Marie suggested. It wasn't the first time she'd done so. Years ago, when Sydney first began to sink under the heavy weight of depression, Marie tried everything. For a while she had been subtle, had stuffed inspirational sayings, scriptures, and self-help articles in hidden places all over Sydney's house. One time she opened the toilet lid and saw a Psalm taped to it. Then she moved on to less subtle methods, began dragging Sydney places to get her out of the house, had a few times physically forced Sydney out of bed and into the sunshine, bundling her onto the back deck in a blanket like an invalid.

Now she was much more resigned. This was the new normal. Sydney was a slug, unable to perform even the most basic functions on most days. And really, she didn't have to. As much as Marie wanted to help, her overbearing enablement meant Sydney didn't have to do anything beyond survive. Supper was made. The house was clean. Laundry was done. Joe was still cocooned by his loving, supportive family. The only thing he needed from Sydney was the one thing she couldn't give him, an heir. If they lived a few hundred years ago, he could have her beheaded for her inability. As it was now she had relegated herself to this sad shell of humanity, alive in only the most basic way. Was it unfair to Joe to withdraw so entirely? Yes. Did she know how to change it? No.

"I've been to lots of doctors," Sydney reminded her, ending on another yawn. So tired. She was so tired.

Marie surprised her by climbing over her and lying down beside her, assuming Joe's regular spot. She stared up at the ceiling as if trying to see what Sydney saw. *What's so great about this bed?* She could almost hear Marie's thoughts.

"Doctors," Marie huffed. "I'm talking about someone who's good with head stuff. A counselor, maybe a pastor or priest. Maybe there's some medicine…"

"I tried the medicine," Sydney interjected. It hadn't made her feel better, hadn't made her feel anything but flat. And she had gained ten pounds, insult to injury after the ten she gained from the fertility meds. "I'm just broken, Marie. It is what it is."

"Nonsense," Marie said, tone vehement. "You are not broken. But you have a lot going on inside you, Peaches. And not just the, er, baby thing." Marie had trouble saying the word "infertile." It was as if she didn't say it, then it wouldn't be true. "Your childhood…"

"Lots of people have rough childhoods and can still have kids," Sydney said. Her sister, for instance, was as fertile as humanly possible.

"But you've never talked to anyone about all the things. It's too much." Marie pressed her fingers to her eyes, a sure sign she was trying hard not to cry. A little bit of feeling broke through Sydney's flat façade and she grimaced.

"Please don't," Sydney whispered, pleading. She couldn't take Marie's feelings on top of all the ones she was trying not to feel herself.

Marie swallowed convulsively a few times, trying to get herself back under control. Sydney turned her face to the window, the heavy weight of guilt and failure now pressing down on her. She hadn't merely failed Joe with her inability to have a child; she had failed Marie as well, and Pete and all the Samperi siblings. All of them would love to see a baby Joe, another too big baby with a heart of gold. Would their baby have Joe's dark hair or her downy fluff? His hazel eyes or her green ones?

She didn't realize she was crying until Marie hugged her. She didn't hug her in return; she couldn't. It was as if her arms were bolted to the bed now. *Failure. You are such a failure.* She had let Joe down, had let his family down, had failed in the one way that mattered most. Who cared that she was smart, a good teacher, a nice person? None of that mattered if she couldn't do this one thing, and she couldn't. It was becoming clear that it would never happen. She was thirty six years old. Even if she'd been fertile, her years of eligibility would be waning. Now it was becoming fantasy. *Broken, broken, broken, broken.* The word rattled through her, poking her from the inside with its sharp edges.

"We love you, Peaches," Marie whispered.

"I love you, too," Sydney dutifully replied. She did love them, of course she did. They had been part of her life since she was twelve years old. But she heard what Marie left unsaid. *We love you even though you're broken. Even though you're a sad lump who doesn't leave her bed. Even though you're a husk of a person now. We love you because we have to, because we're family.* What if they weren't family anymore? What if they weren't tethered by the bonds of matrimony? What if she and Joe cut that tie and Sydney floated free, a lump all on her own, childless and unmarried? *Alone, alone, alone.* In a way she felt as if she was preparing herself for that eventuality. Things with Joe couldn't go on as they had. Someday things between them would come to a head, and then what? *And then I'll be alone, as I've always been, as I was always meant to be.* It seemed inevitable. She had never been good enough to bear the Samperi name. Maybe soon she'd have to give it back.

"Want me to bring you some cannoli?" Marie asked, sitting up to peer down at her. Her face was so hopeful that it tugged a small smile from Sydney's reluctant face. Marie believed everything could be solved with enough food and enough love. Would that it were so.

"No, thank you. I should probably cut back." She should, but she likely wouldn't. She would keep eating herself into oblivion, surrounding herself with an insulating layer of fat to keep the world at bay, to keep the feelings out.

Marie sat up and glanced out the window. Her frustration was palpable. She so badly wanted to fix Sydney. The trouble, Sydney realized, was that she either didn't want to be fixed or was now beyond repair. She didn't know which was worse, and she didn't know which thought would hurt Marie more.

"Well," Marie said, striving for a bright tone, "I'll leave it in the fridge, then. I brought some greens, some scampi, manicotti. All your favorites." She said it as if it were something unusual when, really, it was the same scene on repeat since their early marriage. Sydney had never been given the chance to be a real wife, the kind who made horrible meals until she learned to do better. Mama Samperi had always been there, always swooped in with good food, clean sheets, and a can-do attitude. A tiny sting of resentment festered in Sydney's chest, shocking her with its potency.

"Thank you," she said tightly.

Marie bit her lip, nodded once, eased from the bed and went downstairs. A minute later, Sydney heard the vacuum begin. Marie would vacuum, clean the kitchen, take out the trash, arrange Sydney's life so completely it would be almost as if she didn't exist. Most days she wished she didn't. She should get up, help, tell her to go home. Something. *Anything.* Instead she pulled the pillow over her head and rolled over, cocooning herself in the covers once again.

CHAPTER 5

*J*oe was fairly certain his nose was broken. Again. Worse, Peaches was upset with him.

"You can't keep doing this, Joey," she said as they walked down the long lane toward his home.

"You didn't hear what they were saying," Joe said. It hurt to talk. It would hurt worse after his mother took a look at him and realized he'd been fighting again.

"It doesn't matter," Sydney said.

"It matters to me," Joe said.

She stopped in the middle of the lane, frustrated. "It's not going to stop. There will always be talk about my family because it will always be true."

"It's not true about you," he said. He hated that she so often got caught in the web of her family's misdeeds. Most recently her seventeen-year-old sister got arrested for stealing a car, driving drunk, and crashing into a tree. She was unharmed; the car was not. It was Joe's bad luck he walked into the locker room when two guys were discussing the family's most recent scandal. They saw Joe, and talk turned to Sydney. The things they said about her...it made his fists clench to remember. It hadn't mattered there were two of them any more than it mattered that they were two years older. He matched them in size, and he had anger on his side. It was Joe's bad luck that a third guy joined in, a senior. Together he and one of the guys held Joe down while the third broke his nose. And that was when the principal showed up.

"You got suspended," Sydney said.

"So?"

"So you're covered in blood, and your mom is going to kill you. And then she's going to kill me because it was all my fault."

"It wasn't your fault," Joe protested.

"You wouldn't have gotten into it, if it weren't for me," she said.

"You don't know that. Maybe I would have punched him because I like punching things," he said.

She smiled a little at that, as he knew she would. "You are the sweetest, gentlest person I've ever met."

"Nope, total thug gangster," he said. He dropped his backpack and put his arms around her, pulling her close.

"You cried when your cat's last litter of kittens was stillborn," she reminded him, slipping her arms around his waist.

"That was supposed to be a secret," he said.

"I'll never tell a soul," she promised. She pressed her face to his chest. He kissed the top of her head.

"Why does it make you so mad when I fight for you?" he asked, puzzled.

"Because some day you're going to get tired of it. Someday it's all going to be too much," she said.

"Peaches, why would you even say that?" Joe asked. She shook her head. He put his finger under her chin and tilted her face up. "Why?"

"Look at you. Your nose is permanently crooked because of me," she said.

"So?"

"So it's like a reminder now every time I look at you of what you've had to do for me, because of my family, because of who I am," she said. Her eyes filled with tears again. She brushed them impatiently away. "How many times can you pull me up before you realize it's not worth it?"

Joe didn't know the right words to say, so he said the only thing that made sense. "I love you." They had been together for two years, a friendship that slowly morphed into something more. Their first kiss had only been a few months ago, the summer before freshman year. He had never said the words to her; they came out easier than he would have thought.

"You shouldn't," she said, but she stood on her toes and kissed him until he forgot how much his nose hurt.

"Guess what?" he said when the kiss was finally finished.

"What?"

"My parents said you're invited to Thanksgiving this year in Brooklyn."

"For real?" she asked, excited.

"For real," he said. "But, Peaches, it's not that great. You'll have to sleep on the floor. It's crazy crowded and so loud your ears are going to bleed."

"It's going to be epic," Sydney said, practically dancing with anticipation.

"You know what this means," Joe said. "You're a real Samperi now. Only Samperis are allowed at my grandma's on Thanksgiving."

There was nothing Sydney wanted more than to be an actual part of Joe's family, if only to escape her own dreadful lineage. She bent and picked up his heavy backpack, shoving it into his hands. They began to walk again, hand in hand. "Hey, Joey," she said.

"What?" he asked.

"I love you, too, you know."

"I know." He gave her hand a squeeze and they finished the long walk to his house, hand in hand.

CHAPTER 6

ydney heard Joe's truck in the garage and sat up in alarm. Why was he home so early? She rooted from beneath the covers, paused the television, and dodged into the bathroom, brushing her teeth and scrubbing her face in record time. When that was finished, she swiped on some mascara, arranged her hair into a ponytail, tore off her pajamas, and put on some clothes.

She descended the stairs two at a time and came to a screeching halt in the living room, stopping short at the sight of Joe. *He looks so sad,* she thought, her heart stuttering. He stared off into space, slumped and diminished somehow. *I did this to him,* she thought. She had taken a lion of a man, a great big tender hearted grizzly bear and turned him into this grieving, wilted old man.

"Hey," she said tentatively.

He mustered a smile for her. "Hey. What'd you do today?"

There was no way to tell him she had lain in bed the last ten hours, contemplating life and crying. She shrugged, came forward, and surprised them both by easing into his lap. There was a time when any space between them had felt odd. Now it felt odd to cross over all the invisible barriers. But she couldn't not touch him when he looked so forlorn. He wrapped her tightly in his big arms and drew her close, pressing a kiss to her head. There were moments, like now, when Sydney felt like everything would be okay. They were Joe and Peaches; they would overcome anything.

She pressed her head to his heart, listening to its steady thump, comforted as always. Joe was and had always been her rock. Since she was twelve years old, he had been the person she turned to. When did they start to turn on each other? She hated it, hated what they'd become, but had no idea how to get back out of the hole they'd dug for themselves. His hand eased up and down her spine, and she gave a little shiver. It amazed her how she was always able to respond to him, regardless of anything else. All he had to do was touch her, and she'd melt. But somehow, even knowing that, he hardly touched her anymore. She pressed a kiss to his neck before she could let herself sink too low.

He blew out a breath and threaded his fingers in her hair. "Molly's going to take some time off work."

"Is it that bad?" she asked.

"It's that bad. They're talking about hospitalizing her for a while."

"Oh," Sydney replied, an odd mix of feelings. She felt bad for Molly, of course. The poor sweet girl had to be miserable. But she was also strangely envious of her misery. Sydney would give anything, absolutely anything, to experience what she was experiencing right now. "I can help with Bella."

"I'm sure they'd appreciate that."

"What are you going to do for a secretary?"

Joe blew out a breath. "We'll have to hire someone."

She smiled. That must be the source of his weariness. He hated change, hated upending everything and adding new people into the mix. Her fingers edged under his shirt and she let her fingers glide over his impressive muscles. He was impossibly ripped. His body seemed to grow harder and stronger with the passing years, unlike Sydney who became softer, plumper, a pasty wad of dough. Joe never complained about the unpleasant changes to her body, but sometimes she wondered. How could he possibly still find her attractive when she was so completely diminished?

He caught her wrist and held it. "Peaches."

His tone sounded anguished. She sat up and looked in his face, too frightened now to ask what was wrong.

"They're pregnant," he rasped.

Her heart froze. "Who?"

"All of them. Vivian, Lou, Jessamine. All of them, they're all pregnant."

She jumped off his lap like she'd been electrocuted, stumbling back a step. His hand reached out to her. "Don't go."

She took another step back, dodging his touch. "I need some air." Blindly, she reached for her keys and ran out the door.

CHAPTER 7

"Peaches, this isn't a good idea."

"It's a great idea," Sydney said.

"Let's get down," Joe pled.

"That's what I'm planning to do," Sydney said. She was draped precariously over the side of the bridge.

"I meant let's climb down," Joe said. He tugged her hand. She turned to him with a bright smile, eyes sparkling with adventure.

"Joey, everybody has jumped off this bridge but us. It's going to be fun, you'll see."

"There's a shallow spot right there. If you hit that, you could break something. You could *die*," Joe said.

"Then I'll try not to hit that spot," she said.

She was really going to do it; she was really going to jump from the high train trestle to the water below. Three years together, and he was seeing a new side of her today; his girlfriend craved adventure. Of course he knew she loved roller coasters and was always up for something new and exciting, but he had no idea how enthusiastic she would become at the thought of plummeting two stories off a bridge.

"I'm doing this with or without you. I won't be upset if you don't do it, but I think you'll be upset with yourself if you don't," she said. She slipped her hand onto his shoulder and gave it a squeeze.

She knew exactly how to get to him. Of course he wouldn't let her do it alone, and of course he wouldn't want to have regrets later over not doing it. He climbed over the edge and took her hand. "Together?"

"Together," she said, and they jumped. The plunge was exhilarating. When they emerged, Sydney was laughing.

"That was amazing. Let's do it again," she said.

They did it again. When she wanted to do it a third time, Joe raised the white flag. "I can't climb up there again. Aren't you tired?"

"Are you kidding me? I might never sleep again. It was like jumping out of an airplane, or so I imagine." She grabbed his hand. "Let's jump out of an airplane."

"What?"

"With a parachute, I mean. Or we could bungee jump." She bobbed up and down in the water.

"I don't think they let fifteen year olds do that," Joe said, but he loved her enthusiasm. In the last few months, she had undergone a transition. As the town began to realize she was different from her family, she began to relax and release some of the underlying tension that had accompanied her. Without that, she was all sparkles and excitement, a ray of color and delight in Joe's ordinary life.

"Someday," she implored. "Let's go on adventures. Let's do all our firsts together." She paused and rolled her eyes before he could interrupt. "Except our first kiss. I know you kissed the girl behind Gray's Papaya."

"I heard she's pregnant now," Joe interjected.

"See? No good comes from having your first kiss behind a hot dog vendor," she said.

"What good comes from having your first kiss on a Ferris wheel?" he asked.

"Everything." She tried to kiss him, but they began to sink. They bobbed to the surface again and she tugged his arm. "Come on, one more time and I'll be done. Please, pretty please."

Joe deliberated, as if he had a choice. In reality he couldn't refuse her anything she wanted so badly. "One more time," he reluctantly agreed.

In the end, they jumped three more times, until they were so exhausted they had to crawl up onto the bank and try to regain enough energy for the long walk home. Sydney lay with her face tilted toward the sun, eyes closed, her long blond hair splayed out behind her. Joe lay on his side, watching her. He wished he could take a picture of her. His parents had given him a camera for his fourteenth birthday last year, and ever since he had become almost obsessed with photography. So far he had only shown Sydney his pictures, but she had been encouraging about his "talent," as she called it. Between work and time spent with her, he didn't have much left over for photography, but he was beginning to view everything through a lens. Now he took in the angle of her face and the light that bounced off the rock. The picture would be perfect, but it would have to be a mental snapshot instead.

"You're staring at me," she said.

"You're pretty," he replied. She wrinkled her nose at the compliment. He rolled onto his back and sighed. "It figures that the one time we're actually alone I'm too tired to do anything about it."

"Have you noticed your mom has a sixth sense about whenever we start to make out and one of your brothers or your sister mysteriously appears?" she said.

"Let's test the theory," he said, reaching for her.

"I thought you were out of energy," she said.

"I rallied," he said. He kissed her and, approximately thirty seconds later, his youngest brother, Moss, burst through the bushes.

"I found them, and they're kissing again," Moss yelled. A few seconds later, the rest of his siblings appeared.

"What were you guys doing?" Jessamine asked.

"They were kissing, I told you," Moss said. "Gross."

It was Giovanni who made the connection between their location and the train trestle. He gasped. "You jumped off the bridge."

"Joe," Benny admonished in the same tone as their mother. "Mom said you're not allowed to."

"She said it wasn't a good idea; she never said I wasn't allowed," Joe informed them.

"I want to do it," Jessamine said.

"Me, too," Moss added.

"Of course you do, but you're five," Joe said. He stood and put a hand down for Peaches. "No one is jumping off the bridge."

"You did," Giovanni accused.

"I'm older. When you're fifteen, you can do it too," Joe said. "What are you guys doing here anyway?"

"Ma sent us to find you," Moss said. "She said we needed to find you before you got into trouble. She must know about the bridge."

"Yes, Moss," Benny said. He put his arm around his little brother and steered him away. "Ma was definitely talking about the bridge."

"Sixth sense," Joe said, shaking his head in frustration.

"She's only looking out for us," Sydney said.

"Sure she is," Joe said. "I can't get any freedom or privacy."

"I have all the freedom and privacy I want," Sydney said. Her parents couldn't care less where she was or what she did. "It's not all it's cracked up to be. You are loved."

"I am smothered," he said.

"I would give anything to be smothered," Sydney said.

"Be careful what you wish for," Joe said. He put his arm around her and, with his siblings, began the long walk home.

CHAPTER 8

$\mathcal{S}$ ydney drove with no destination in mind for a long time,
around and around and around their small town until,
eventually, she parked by the river. She imagined loading her pockets
with boulders and walking into the river, letting the water flood over
her while she closed her eyes and waited for death. It was a beautiful
daydream, an end to the pain and misery her life had become. But
always there was Joe to consider. Being married to her had caused
him untold amounts of pain and suffering, but committing suicide
would kill him. As much as she wanted an end to her own pain, she
couldn't, *wouldn't* do that to him. Ever, no matter what. She told
herself repeatedly until she was able to turn away from the river and
banish the daydream. *Suck it up, Sydney. Suicide is for quitters.*

She crossed her arms over her body and squeezed, trying to hold
herself together. How could she possibly continue to function when
everything hurt so badly? Her early life, before Joe, had been a nightmare, a black hole of despair. And then he burned onto the scene like
a comet, lifting her, rescuing her, lighting her world. With him she'd
felt invincible. For a few years she'd felt such hope, such happiness
and joy. And then they started trying to have children and everything
became as it was, black, bleak, failure. Her fault, all her fault.

There was no official diagnosis for their infertility. *Unexplained* was a terrible word. She longed for an explanation, a definition. Not knowing was almost as bad as knowing because, regardless, Sydney blamed herself. She was a woman; it was her lot in life to birth babies. Absolutely everyone could do it but her. Her body had betrayed her in the worst possible way, and now she was thirty six. She would likely never have a baby, never give Joe his much longed for child. It was the one thing she was supposed to be able to do for him, the one way in which she could somehow try to repay him for all he'd done for her, and she had let him down. Shame washed over her in suffocating sheets.

Failure, you are a miserable failure. You can't even be a woman correctly. It was all you had, and now you failed that, too.

And now every one of her sisters-in-law was pregnant, all four of them. Sydney's glaring deficiency would be even more on display. Or, worse, everyone would now tiptoe around her like the damaged goods she was. She could picture an endless string of family events, everyone exclaiming over all the babies and then their eyes landing on Sydney, filled to the brim with pity for her and Joe.

She had no idea she was crying until the cop car arrived. Hastily she wiped her cheeks and tried to push the tears back inside, but they wouldn't go. Worse, the cop was someone she knew, someone from her and Joe's class.

"Peaches?" he said and she laughed. Everyone called her Peaches. That was how closely allied her identity was with Joe's, it had suffused everything. Sydney loved it, had always relished the escape it provided. It was so much better to be Peaches Samperi than Sydney Parker.

"Hi, Cassius," she said, sniffling. He reached into his glove box and handed her a tissue.

"You doing okay? Dumb question, Cassius, of course not. How can I help you?" he amended, his eyes lowering in kind concern.

She shook her head, unable to speak as the tears continued their assault on her face, coursing down her cheeks in streams. She longed for Joe then. How badly she wanted him to hold her in his big, strong arms, to hear him murmur words of love and affirmation. *It's going to be okay, we'll get through this.* Why had she left him? Why did she always walk away when she was hurting most? But she knew the answer to that question. It was because she still believed, even after all these years, that he would someday get tired of coming to her rescue. A man could only be a savior for so long. Eventually he had to grow weary. Joe was long overdue for giving up on her.

"Do you want me to call Joe?" Cassius asked.

She shook her head furiously. That was all she needed, for him to get a call from their former classmate. *Come get your crazy wife. She's having some kind of public breakdown at the river.* It was likely what Joe was waiting for, what everyone was waiting for. Poor Sydney who can't handle life and cries all the time.

She leaned against the car and tried to take a deep breath. She was so tired of being broken, so tired of grieving and being sad. Cassius leaned beside her, sharing her space, sharing her grief. And somehow, it helped. She was able to push the tears away, at least for the time being. She took a few shuddering breaths and cleared her throat.

"What do you do when you're sad, Cassius?" she asked, apropos of nothing. Or possibly apropos of everything. He stared thoughtfully into the distance, tilting his head.

"I hit the gym."

"I could stand to hit the gym," Sydney admitted, pinching a roll of fat on her belly. She had taken so much infertility medicine over the years. Some of the medicine made her a bubbling cauldron of crazy, raging hormones. Some of it made her unendingly hungry. She had turned to food as a way to soothe the pain and ease the hunger. It had helped with the hunger, but not the pain. And it left her twenty pounds overweight.

"Nah, you look good," Cassius said easily. "Believe me, I'm on Tinder. You're leaps and bounds above any of them. You look like that girl you were, our former homecoming queen." He elbowed her.

She wrinkled her nose up at him. "What are you doing on Tinder?"

He cleared his throat and adjusted his vest. "Sherry and I got divorced."

She stood up away from the car. "What? I didn't hear that. I'm so sorry, Cassius."

He gave her a sad smile. "It's happened to most of us. You and Joe seem to be the only ones who can go the distance."

Frowning now, she turned toward the river. Cassius didn't comment on her frown. "You sure I can't call him for you?"

She shook her head, forcing a smile. "I'm okay. Bad night, I guess."

"Everyone has those," he said kindly. "Doesn't mean anything, in the long run. The good always outweighs the bad."

She nodded, pretending to believe him. "Thanks Cassius. You take care."

He opened her door and waited for her to get inside before speaking. "You too, Syd." He closed the door and watched her drive away, a concerned frown still on his face.

CHAPTER 9

*J*oe sat up and held his breath. His brothers and sister were finally asleep. Every year it seemed to take longer for them to nod off. On the opposite side of the room, Sydney sat up and smiled at him. He stood and began picking his way between the bodies, careful not to step on anyone or make a noise. At last he reached his destination and lay down, sandwiched between Sydney and the wall.

"How are you holding up?" he whispered. They were smashed together on the floor of his grandmother's living room. It was Peaches' third Thanksgiving in Brooklyn with the family.

"Why do you always ask me that?" she replied.

"You've got to be on Samperi overload," he said.

"I love your family," she said. "I never get tired of them."

"Oh, Peaches, you've gone delirious," he said.

She giggled and covered her mouth with her hand. On her other side, Moss snorted and rolled over. His six-year-old brother was as attached to her as Joe was, but for vastly different reasons. Moss had no remembrance of life before Peaches. To him, she was like another sister. All of his siblings regarded her as one of the family, as did his parents, and even his grandmother. And Nonna was a notoriously tough customer. He took her hand and kissed it.

"Hey, Peaches."

"What?"

"Marry me."

"We're sixteen," she reminded him.

"Marry me someday," he amended.

"I thought that was already a given," she said.

"Let's make it unofficially official," he said.

"All right," she agreed. He loved that, even after four years together, she could still sound shy sometimes. He kissed her. When the kiss was finished, much sooner than he would have preferred, she snuggled down into his embrace.

"Joey."

"Hmm." He was falling asleep. Was she going to tell him to go back to his side of the room? His mother and grandmother would keel over if they caught him out of bed and by her side in the darkened room.

"I love it here."

"I'm glad," he said.

"No, I mean I really, really love it here. I love Brooklyn. I think I'm a big city kind of girl. I could never get tired of this. Don't you miss living here?"

"Kentucky has certain benefits," he said, giving her a squeeze.

"Let's live here when we get married," she said and Joe's eyes popped open.

"What?" he said.

"Let's live here. I'll go to college and you can go to art school and study photography. We'll be insanely poor but happy. We can take the subway and get Chinese food every day. We'll go to museums and the park and complain about traffic and how crazy everyone is. Please, Joe, please." She clutched his shirt and danced a little in her sleeping bag.

"Um," Joe said, stalling. Was she serious? She knew how it was, that he was already bound to take over the family business. Benny had been given the OK to go away and be a missionary, but his dad couldn't afford to let any more kids go. Joe was already practically working full time to help him keep up, and even Jessamine had been given a hammer and enlisted to meet the growing demand. "I don't know, Peaches."

"Don't you want to?" she asked, sounding slightly hurt.

"I would live with you anywhere, you know that. A rat-infested hut in the Indian Ocean would be fine with me, even if we got typhoid fever from the rats. But where we live might not be up to me, you know? Anything could happen between now and then."

"That's kind of an exciting thought too, isn't it? Anything could happen in our lives. Who knows what amazing thing might be out there for us? When your parents got married, I bet they never envisioned having so many kids or moving halfway across the country to start over."

He smoothed his hand down her arm. Part of him wanted to promise their lives would be an exciting adventure. The more pragmatic side of him realized that probably wouldn't be true. And the insecure part of him wondered if what he could offer her would ever be enough.

CHAPTER 10

In the end, Sydney went home. She had nowhere else to go. She both hoped and feared Joe's reaction to her arrival. Would it be anger, pity, or frustration? It was none of those things. He was in bed, either asleep or pretending to be. Somewhere along the way she'd lost the ability to tell. She stripped, slid into her pajamas, and eased into bed beside him, longing for his touch. When it didn't come, she sidled closer, pressing her body against his, trying to steal his reassurance by osmosis.

In the morning it was her turn to pretend to be asleep when he kissed her cheek goodbye and slipped out of the house. She reached for the remote and froze. *No.* She could not, would not spend one more day in this bed wallowing in grief and self-pity, especially not when it was what everyone now expected her to do. *Oh, all her sisters-in-law are pregnant? This is going to break her. Poor Peaches.* She was so tired of being Poor Peaches. Plus her mother-in-law was coming again today to load their refrigerator and pick up the laundry.

In the beginning, when Sydney was a young wife and new teacher, she had dearly appreciated her mother-in-law's help in that regard. Teaching was exhausting; teaching kindergarten was like being a zookeeper to animals that had no cages. Life had been a blur back then, and it had been an unmitigated relief to have Mama Samperi step in and handle the cooking and laundry. And now, fifteen years later, it was…well, it was best not to peer too closely at what it was. All she knew was that she didn't want to be there when her mother-in-law arrived, didn't want to receive a hug or hear a rousing lecture or anything else Marie Samperi had to say about a situation that was absolutely none of her business. Not today when Sydney was still trying to absorb the shock of all of her family being pregnant at once.

Sydney tossed off the covers and dressed in her workout clothes. She put her hair up, applied a dab of makeup, and left the house. Leaving the house during summer was so unusual that she already felt refreshed. During the school year, her schedule kept her functioning. She had to get up every day and go to work. During the summer, she cocooned, burrowing into the covers and not seeing the sunlight for days and weeks at a time.

She headed across town to her friend Chrissy's apartment. Chrissy looked the least like a Chrissy as was humanly possible. She looked, well, Sydney hated to even think it, but she looked like a toad—short squat, crew cut hair, bulgy eyes, and round middle. They were possibly the least likely pairing on the planet, and yet Chrissy was the best girl friend Sydney had ever had. It helped that she hadn't grown up in town, knew nothing of Sydney's family or her relationship with the Samperis, outside what Sydney had told her. But it was more than that. Chrissy always said exactly what was on her mind, had no people pleasing tendencies whatsoever. Sydney admired that, desperately envied the frankness other people found off-putting. It was likely Chrissy had as few other friends as Sydney did, but for vastly differing reasons. Sydney had been popular in high school, but she had never warmed up to anyone in her group, never trusted them completely, never certain if they were only pretending to like her and would turn on her and hurt her. Joe and his family had been her only real friends until Chrissy came along. Chrissy simply didn't like people. She was a self-avowed misanthrope, Sydney being the only exception to her no-people rule.

They were the kind of friends who didn't have to provide a

warning call before they showed up unannounced at each other's houses. When Chrissy did it to Sydney, she never found it unexpectedly messy. Even wallowing in unending depression, Sydney kept a tidy house, building on Marie's hard work of cleaning. Chrissy, on the other hand…

"Oh, hey, come in," Chrissy said, turning her back and leading the way inside, picking her path around piles of laundry, books, and trash. Sydney, who couldn't stand to visit her parents because they were so messy and gross, didn't even wrinkle her nose. She couldn't care less if Chrissy was messy, wouldn't mind at all if she one day turned into a desperate hoarder who had to be cut out of her house. Chrissy had given her an open, honest, and trustworthy love; Sydney would do nothing less in return. "What's up?"

"All my sisters-in-law are pregnant."

Chrissy faced her and said a dirty, naughty word Sydney would never say, but somehow it made her feel better to hear Chrissy say it on her behalf. Chrissy had zero desire for marriage or children. She was happy exactly as she was, but she knew Sydney's heart and didn't judge her for it. Her sympathy was real and deep and also lacking pity. She sank to a chair at her overloaded kitchen table. "I'm sorry, Syd."

"Me, too. But I'm tired of being sorry, Chrissy. It's time to be proactive."

"You want to go Thelma and Louise? I can be packed and ready in five minutes," Chrissy said.

"No, I want to join a gym."

"Get out."

Sydney laughed. "I'm serious, and of course I'll pay for you to join with me." She had nothing else to do with her money. It was an irony that, after growing up in extreme poverty, she now had money coming out her ears and absolutely no one to spend it on. When she was a kid, she swore to herself she would one day make enough money to pay for her kids' college educations outright. Now she and Joe had three fully funded accounts with no names attached.

"A gym?" Chrissy said, grimacing. "All those men."

Chrissy was terrified of men, and rightly so. She had been abused in the worst possible ways by a series of her mother's boyfriends, as well as an uncle and a few cousins. It didn't take a psychologist to see why her friend had made herself as un-feminine as possible. "Hey, no one is going to hurt you with me around," Sydney said, giving her hand a squeeze. Sydney was probably the only person Chrissy allowed to touch her, and she did it often, bestowing the same swallowing hugs she bestowed on her kindergarteners. And Chrissy reacted the same way, soaking up the affection and letting it settle in her most exposed spots.

"All right," Chrissy reluctantly agreed, as Sydney knew she would. They were there for each other, always and in all the ways. Only two people who had survived the sort of childhood trauma they had could understand how deep the bond went. Neither trusted many people, but once they did, they opened up completely. The bond went deep, and it would go forever.

Chrissy changed, and they headed for the gym. They got looks wherever they went together. Their unlikely pairing seemed to confuse people. Sydney was a girly girl who, even in the midst of a deep and lasting depression, took the time to do her hair and makeup, to select stylish and matching clothing. Chrissy looked like she grabbed the first thing she saw and threw it on, which she undoubtedly had, and put zero effort into her overtly boyish appearance. People could never figure out the draw between them, and Sydney didn't care. She edged protectively closer to Chrissy, trying to deflect the looks heading her way. Why did people have to be so nasty? Why did they have to pass judgment with their expressions? Why couldn't the world be kind?

"I'm going to try running," Sydney said. She used to be a runner, back in the day when she'd been head cheerleader. A lifetime ago.

"I'm not," Chrissy said and Sydney snorted a laugh. They nabbed adjoining treadmills, tuning the television before them to the Food network, a combined favorite. Chrissy set her treadmill to the lowest possible setting, not even pretending to break a sweat. Sydney started out slow and worked her way up to a brisk run. To her surprise and delight, it felt good to be running again. She wasn't certain if her body was hungry for exercise or if she was merely so delighted to be doing anything but wallowing in misery. For whatever reason, she felt flooded in endorphins for the first time in a long, long time.

CHAPTER 11

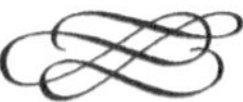

*S*ydney crouched in the hall, hands over her ears. Her parents were fighting again, and she wasn't sure what to do. In the past when she'd called the police, they had punished her after her father was released from jail. He wouldn't hit her again; Joe was big enough and powerful enough now that her father was afraid of him. But they had other ways of hurting her.

If he started hitting her mom, she would have to call, even if it made her mother angry. When a knock sounded on the door, Sydney braced, torn between tension and relief. Had a neighbor already called the police? If so, would her parents believe it had been the neighbor and not her? They didn't hear the knock, so intent were they on their fight. Her mom shoved her dad, signaling that things were about to become physical. Sydney skirted by them and flung open the door.

"Hi, dear, I know you have that pep rally tomorrow, so I washed your uniform." Joe's mother stood on the doorstep, Sydney's cheerleading uniform held aloft.

"Oh, thank you," Sydney said, cheeks flaming. She stepped forward and pinched the door closed behind her, hoping to shield Mrs. Samperi from the sounds coming from behind her.

No such luck, though. Mrs. Samperi's eyes skittered behind her, narrowing. "Is everything okay, dear?"

Sydney swallowed hard, hating to lie and yet knowing she had no choice. "Everything is fine, thank you, Mrs. Samperi." She reached for her uniform. Mrs. Samperi snatched it back.

"I think I'll have a word with your parents while I'm here."

"Oh, no, please, don't, no…" Sydney pled, but it was too late. Mrs. Samperi snaked by her, pushed open the door, and charged inside. For a second, Sydney stood frozen, hands pressed over her eyes. Mrs. Samperi would see, would know how horrible the truth of Sydney's life was. And then a new horror struck. What if her dad hurt Mrs. Samperi? What if he killed her? Joe would never forgive her for that, no one would. Panicked now, Sydney sprinted inside, skidding to a halt in the living room where the three adults stood staring at each other in tense silence, three corners of a hostile triangle.

"Is there a problem?" Mrs. Samperi said. By her tone, Sydney thought it wasn't the first time she'd voiced the question.

"None of your business. Get out," her father said, pointing toward the door.

"I hardly think this is an appropriate way to behave in front of Peaches," Mrs. Samperi said.

Her mother scowled. "That's not her name."

Mrs. Samperi faced her, her formidable features making her seem taller somehow. "That's our name for her."

"She's not yours," her mother continued, turning her wrath from Sydney's father to Mrs. Samperi. "She doesn't belong to you. She belongs to us."

"She's not a possession," Mrs. Samperi said, voice low and dangerous. "But we love her as if she were one of our own children." Her gaze bounced between Sydney's parents. "I don't think it's appropriate or safe for her to remain here tonight." She turned to Sydney. "Get your things, dear. You're coming with me."

"Oh, no she isn't," her mother said, taking a threatening step forward.

Mrs. Samperi took her own step forward and her mother cowered, actually cowered at the look on her face. "Oh, yes she is. You want to know why? Because I've noted every bruise and scratch that has ever appeared on this child. I dated each one, and then you know what I did? I contacted Children's Services and my lawyer. It's all on record, all of it. We've already started custody proceedings."

Sydney was shocked, no, *floored.* She had no idea Joe's parents knew about the way her parents sometimes smacked her when they were angry, and certainly no idea they had plans to do anything about it. Joe had never said a word. She wondered if he even knew.

Her mother was shaking with rage now. She hated to think of anyone having anything rightfully hers. Her father looked frightened. He already had a record. Getting arrested for domestic violence was one thing; getting picked up for child abuse wasn't quite as easy to squirm out of. "Hey, now," he said, trying to inject some calm into the situation, an irony since he was such an angry, volatile drunk. *So apparently you can turn it off and on, Dad, based on how it will affect you. Good to know.*

"She's our kid," her mother said, voice low and shaky with anger. "You cannot take her."

"Watch me," Mrs. Samperi said. "Sydney, pack a bag," she commanded without turning to look at her.

Her mother looked at her. "You can't take anything. You want to go with them, you leave it all behind. And don't come back."

Mrs. Samperi turned to face her now but, unlike her mother, her face was filled with love and kindness. "Is there anything you can't leave without, dear?"

The things she wanted most were the things Joe had given her, notes, cards, little gifts, a stuffed bear. But if she left now, she would have Joe and his family. She shook her head. Mrs. Samperi held out her hand. Sydney put her shaking one in her grasp, finding it warm and solid. Mrs. Samperi gave her a reassuring squeeze and smile. "Let's go home, Peaches," she said. She turned and tugged Sydney toward the door. Sydney followed her without a backwards glance.

CHAPTER 12

"They're horrible, all horrible," Giovanni groaned, his eyes squeezed tightly closed.

"I'm sorry," Moss said with unaccustomed humility.

"It's not your fault your wife is sick," Giovanni said. It was such a rare moment of peace and grace between them. No one spoke for a few minutes, letting it linger.

"We have one more candidate," Jessamine said. She aimed for hopefulness, but couldn't quite pull it off. They'd been interviewing interim secretaries all morning, to their combined horror. So far every one seemed either crazy or incompetent, which wasn't so surprising. They needed someone for a few weeks. What kind of person was able to take on a fulltime job for such a short amount of time? Crazy people, apparently. Thanks to their new notoriety and television show, they'd had a lot of candidates, a thousand, to be exact. Molly, sick as she was, had spent the last few days culling the herd, trying to pick the best possible candidates. She somehow narrowed it down to a dozen, but so far every single one of them had been a dud.

"Did the third one have a gun in her pocket, or was that my imagination?" Benny asked.

"It was a squirt gun," Joe said. "I saw her pull it out and squirt it into her mouth. Pretty sure it was moonshine." He swiped a hand over his face, wishing the dreadful day was over. Though going home didn't actually hold much appeal, either. Not like the old days when he couldn't wait to get home, couldn't wait to pick up Sydney, to kiss and hold her, giddy with the knowledge that they were finally, officially married. Back then he'd been her hero, the center of her life. And now...he shook his head, pushing dreary thoughts away in order to focus. "Where we at here?"

"Samantha Rogers," Giovanni said, skimming the itinerary in front of him. He had been keeping meticulous notes on each candidate, for whatever it was worth. None of them held out hope for Samantha, but she entered the room as if on a breeze. All of them sat up and took a deep breath. She was young, twenties probably, dressed professionally with a pleasant smile on a pretty face. She sat and made eye contact with each of them before offering a greeting.

"Good afternoon," Joe said. As the de facto head of the company, he was also in charge of the interviews.

"Good afternoon," Samantha said, her voice soft and pleasant. Her smile never wavered, causing Joe to believe she was not only pleasant but had a fair amount of confidence, a necessity with so many large personalities involved. He ran through his series of questions and she hit each one out of the park. Even if her answers had only been mediocre, she still would have blown everyone else out of the water. He didn't have to look at his siblings to know what the consensus was.

"How soon can you start, Miss Rogers?" he asked at the end of the interview.

"Immediately, Mr. Samperi," she replied, smiling.

"Call me Joe."

"Call me Sam."

They shared a smile, eyes lingering, and Joe looked down, flustered. He wasn't used to women who weren't his wife or sisters, had no idea what to do with them, usually avoided them entirely. It would be odd to have someone not Molly in the office. Thankfully, he was hardly ever there. He breathed a little sigh of relief. He was certain Samantha Rogers would work out fine for the few weeks she'd be there, then Molly would return and all would be well. *Sam,* his mind amended. *Call her Sam.*

CHAPTER 13

"This year's homecoming queen is," their principal paused dramatically before he made the announcement. "Sydney Parker."

Everyone swiveled to look at Sydney. Joe elbowed her. "That's you, Peaches." She shook her head. Clearly there had been some mistake. No one would vote for stinky, white trash Sydney Parker for homecoming queen of their school. Joe took her hand and tugged her forward, handing her off to the principal as if he were giving her away at their wedding. *Wait, it's supposed to be the other way around,* she thought, feeling bereft without Joe's reassuring touch. The principal led her forward while her school counselor placed a crown on her head and a new sash over the one that declared her princess. They backed up, waiting for Sydney to give a reply.

"Gosh, thanks," she squeaked, and everyone laughed. Cassius Carter was crowned homecoming king and they had to take a turn dancing together.

"Congratulations, Peaches. No one deserves this more than you," Cassius whispered sweetly. Sydney shook her head, unable to reply. She could only hope her forced smile looked shocked instead of rude.

The dance finished and Cassius handed her off to Joe. Instead of leading her back onto the floor for another dance, he kept her hand and dragged her behind him, tugging her outside. Once the door was safely closed, he surrounded her with an enveloping embrace and pulled her close. She pressed her face to his chest and wept.

"Why did they do that?" she kept asking.

"Because you're the most beautiful girl in the room, the school, the world," Joe murmured.

She shook her head. "They shouldn't have done that," was all she could say.

He pushed her away from him and cupped her face. "Peaches, look at me."

With effort, she opened her eyes and faced him, flinching at all the love directed toward her. His eyes were so tender, so proud, so filled to the brim with adoration. What had she ever done in her life to deserve someone like him? Nothing, absolutely nothing.

"You are not that dirty little girl from a messed up home. You are smart and beautiful and kind. Absolutely everyone who knows you loves you. Your heart is massive and overflowing. You're going to go to college and become a teacher and change the lives of everyone you encounter. We'll have a million kids and you'll be the best mom in the entire world."

"As good as your mom?" she sniffled.

He smiled. "Better."

She shook her head. "No one is better than your mom. She's the best."

"You'll be better, and we'll have six kids to prove it."

She laughed. "What are you doing with a mess like me, Joe? I'm a wreck."

"You're the most wonderful and amazing and beautiful girl in the entire world, and if you don't stop saying bad things about my favorite person, I'm going to get mad."

"I can't imagine you mad," she said. They'd never so much as exchanged a harsh word. They would be mushy in love forever, she was certain.

He kissed her forehead. "I love you, Syd. So, so much. You're my whole world." He gave her a hard squeeze. "Now, let's go dance because I'm pretty bad at it and we'll likely only have prom as a practice session before our wedding." He took a step toward the school, but she tugged him back.

"You're my best friend, Joe, in addition to being the love of my life."

"Don't forget we're also roommates," he said, and she giggled.

"Scandalous," she said. She stood on her toes and kissed him proper, until he was breathless and leaning on the wall for support.

"How come you don't do that at home?" he asked.

"Because I never want your mother to think I'm taking advantage of her hospitality," she replied, aiming for a prim tone, hard to do when her lips were swollen and one half of her hair had escaped its updo. She tried to smooth it. He shooed her hands away and plucked out the clasp.

"Joe, I'm going to look a right mess," she complained, lunging for the clip.

He held it away from her. "It's okay, you already won. Besides, I love your hair down and curly like this."

"This is how I wear it every day," she said.

"I know, and I love it." He pressed his lips to her neck and kissed her.

"You're supposed to wear it up for homecoming," she said, breathless and halfhearted.

He pulled back and stroked his finger on her cheek. "Most beautiful girl in the world," he whispered.

Just for a moment, she believed him.

CHAPTER 14

"Maybe I'm an addict," Sydney said as she lay on a bench hefting oversized weights over her head. Chrissy stood above her, acting as reluctant and halfhearted spotter. If Sydney did drop the weights on herself, it was highly unlikely Chrissy would notice, enthralled as she was in the television above her. It was their tenth day in a row at the gym. Now that she had made a return to physical fitness, she couldn't seem to get enough.

"You don't even drink," Chrissy said, her gaze never leaving the TV.

"Maybe I'm addicted to exercise," Sydney said.

"Psycho hose beast," Chrissy muttered. Sydney snorted a laugh, nearly strangling herself when the heavy weight collapsed on her neck. As predicted, Chrissy didn't notice. It was Cassius who dodged forward and saved her from the pending catastrophe.

"Peaches?" he exclaimed, easily hefting the weight off her before returning it to the rack.

"Oh, hey, Cassius." She reached for her towel and dabbed her sweaty forehead as she sat up. "I decided to take your suggestion."

He blinked at her. "Really? Mine? You did? Okay."

Behind her, Chrissy snorted like a perturbed bull. Cassius's gaze shifted from Sydney to Chrissy, his look morphing to one of confusion. "Is Joe here?"

Sydney chuckled. "Of course not. He gets his muscles on the job. I came with my best friend. This is Chrissy." She reached out an arm, hugging Chrissy's waist. Chrissy's expression didn't change, but she leaned into the hug a little, absorbing the affection.

"Okay. Well, I'm here a lot. Maybe we could grab a coffee sometime."

"Sure we could," Chrissy preempted, and Cassius's alarmed gaze returned to her.

"Great, really. Great. See you around, Peaches. Christy," he added with a belated nod.

"It's Chrissy," Sydney called.

"He doesn't care," Chrissy said unconcernedly. "Also you know he was hitting on you just then. That coffee invitation was meant for you alone, which was why I intervened. Call me the infidelity police."

Sydney laughed. "What? No way. Cassius has known me forever, since before Joe. He wouldn't be interested in me that way, he knows how it is."

"Syd, he was hitting on you. And you need to tell Joe about this."

"Why would I do that?" Sydney said, feeling squirmy inside, a giveaway that Chrissy was probably correct. Cassius had always been one of the nicer looking guys she'd known. Age had done nothing to diminish that and, in fact, he'd only grown more handsome.

"Because you're vulnerable right now and things between you and Joe aren't exactly roses and sunshine."

Sydney blew out a breath. "Yeah, you're right. I'll tell him." Tears filled her eyes and she sniffed. "How did I get here?"

"Come on," Chrissy said, tugging her bicep. "You can use the spin bike while I sit on the floor and watch *The Barefoot Contessa*."

"You're a really good friend," Sydney said, hugging her again.

"Yeah, well, you'll do, too," Chrissy said, giving her arm a pat. Sydney gave her another squeeze and let her go, hopping onto the spin bike. She felt someone's eyes on her and didn't have to turn to know it was Cassius. For the remainder of their time at the gym, she kept her gaze focused solely on Ina Garten on TV.

*L*ater that night when Joe let himself in, one of his favorite smells greeted him.

"Peach pie," he said, standing in the doorway of the kitchen. Peaches stood at the stove wearing a dress and an apron. His breath caught and his heart stuttered. He would never not be amazed by her beauty, by her easy grace. She gave him a smile and his heart turned over.

"Hey," she said in the same soft, southern drawl that first stole his heart.

"Hey," he returned. He went forward and kissed her, a perfunctory peck. She pulled him back, stood on her toes, and kissed him like she meant it. He backed her against the counter and lifted her and they became aware the oven was beeping.

"My peaches are burning," she murmured.

"I'll say they are," he replied and they laughed, lips together. He let her go and she took supper from the oven. "Good day?"

"Good day," she replied. "Chrissy and I have been going to a gym."

"Chrissy's been going to the gym?" he asked, incredulous.

"They have cable," she replied.

"Ah, Ina Garten to the rescue."

"We ran into Cassius Carter."

"Oh, yeah? What's he up to? Still a cop?"

"Still a cop. He and Sherry got divorced."

"Ah, man. That's horrible, I'm sorry to hear it." He sighed and sat down. "I don't know how that happens."

"How what happens?"

"People getting divorced after all this time. What's the point?"

Sydney didn't reply. Joe didn't seem to notice. "Did I tell you the new girl has a kid?"

"No, is she married?"

He shook his head. "The kid's adorable, though. I happened to stop in the office when her babysitter brought her by. She's three, natural curls. So cute."

"Hmm," Sydney replied. "I've been thinking about something."

"What?"

"I should probably give everyone a baby shower."

He set down his fork. "Why would you do that?"

"Because it's the right thing to do. And who else could? I'm the only one who's not pregnant." The words hurt, badly, but she powered through them.

"Syd, you don't have to do that."

"I'm tired of being a victim."

"A victim of what?" he asked.

"Circumstance, I guess. There goes poor, infertile Sydney. Bless her heart."

"No one thinks less of you because you can't have kids," he said.

"Absolutely everyone thinks less of me because I can't have kids. They're all whispering, wondering what's wrong with me," she said.

"That's paranoid crazy talk. No one cares, except to be sad for us," he said.

Her eyes snapped. "Don't call me paranoid and crazy, Joe."

"Then don't be paranoid and crazy, Sydney."

"You aren't there, you don't hear the things people say."

"No, but I know how sensitive you are. I know you can sometimes misconstrue people's words in the worst possible way."

"Oh, okay, so when your cousin's wife cornered me at that funeral and said I couldn't have kids because there was too much estrogen in my milk when I was a kid, was that me being paranoid and over-sensitive?"

"She's crazy, everyone knows that," he said.

"You don't know, Joe. You don't know what it's like to have the weight of responsibility for our infertility."

"No one knows why we can't have kids."

"No, but that doesn't stop them from blaming me. Clearly it's because I'm defective." Her throat closed, cutting off her words.

He blew out a breath and ran his hand through his hair. "Can't we just move on from it?" he asked softly.

"How, Joe? Please, tell me how. How do I let go of the only dream I've ever had? How do I get over not being able to do something everyone else can do as easily as breathing? I'm honestly asking you how."

"I don't know, but…"

"But what," she pressed.

He looked her in the eye. "I'm so tired of living like this."

She didn't say anything; she couldn't because the thing she feared the most had finally come true. He was tired of her, of trying to fix her broken, messy pieces.

They finished their meal in silence. Sydney cleaned up while Joe turned on a game and fell asleep in front of the TV. She pretended to read a book while he went upstairs to shower. When she crawled into bed sometime later, he pretended to be asleep and she let him. Again.

CHAPTER 15

"What are you hiding?"

Sydney jumped and spun. "Nothing."

Joe came forward and wrapped his arms around her. "Peaches."

"Joe."

"Who has been your best friend and boyfriend for five years?"

"Why, you have, Joseph Samperi."

"Right, so I know you shoved something in that drawer. Do you want to do this the easy way or the hard way?"

"The hard way sounds intriguing," she said.

Grinning, he picked her up and set her on the counter in front of him. She loved it that he was a bear of a guy. His height and breadth made her feel safe. Joe would always be there to fight the bad guys. Sydney's life had taught her there would always be bad guys. She tried to use her legs to hold the drawer closed, but he easily opened it, plucked out the letter she had hastily stuffed away, and scanned it. His expression went from amused to shocked.

"Syd, you got into Duke. I didn't even know you applied to Duke."

"Mr. Applegate pressured me into it." Their guidance counselor had insisted she apply to a few schools, despite her insistence her path was set at the University of Kentucky. She'd be able to live at home.

She and Joe could get married in two years, like they'd always planned.

"Duke. Baby, that's amazing."

"It's not that big of a deal," she said, blushing. She grabbed the letter out of his fingers and stuffed it back in the drawer.

"It's a huge deal. We have to tell Mom and Dad about this."

"No, Joey, please, *please.* I don't want them to know."

"Why not?"

"Because I'm not going to go, obviously."

"Why obviously?" he asked.

"Uh, hello." She pointed between them. He rolled his eyes.

"Peaches, this is *Duke* . You have to at least consider it."

"I could never afford it," she murmured, twisting the hem of her shirt.

"I'm sure you qualify for financial aid," he said.

"My parents would never sign off on that."

"Then my parents will," he said.

She shook her head. "There would still be room and board and books and gas to get places, along with all the other expenses. I can't, I just can't, Joe."

"What is this really about?" he asked.

Her eyes filled with tears. "I don't want to leave you. I can't imagine going one day without seeing you, let alone four years."

"Syddie, we'll be fine. We'll still have our summers and holidays. I'll come visit, and you'll come home. We'll talk on the phone every night." He kissed both cheeks. Sydney couldn't figure out how to explain it. For him, Duke sounded like the obvious choice, a fun new adventure. For Sydney, who had finally found a place and purpose, it sounded like having everything ripped away again. She didn't want to leave him or his family or even their house. For the first time in her life, she finally felt secure. She woke each day unafraid, her belly full, her bed and body clean. Joe, who had never lived any other way, had no idea what a luxury those things were.

His parents were equally ecstatic, and then more shocking news arrived. When Sydney tried to protest it was too much money, they revealed they had been keeping a college account in her name for years. It was plenty enough to pay for Duke, after the scholarships and aid she'd receive. Stunned, she sat still and stared, tears coursing down her cheeks. There was no way out of it; she was going to Duke.

And then a new thought occurred. *Maybe they want me to go away.* Maybe Duke was a convenient way of getting her out of their house, out of their hair. They had five children, why would they want one more? The Samperis were a cohesive unit; they hadn't needed an interloping stranger to mess everything up.

"I'm so proud of you, Peaches," Joe said, picking her up for approximately the twentieth time and giving her a swallowing hug. "My girl, so smart, so hardworking. So hot." He added the last part on a whisper his mother couldn't overhear.

"Look out, Duke, here I come," she said, trying to sound cheerful and excited, trying to hide her absolute dread.

CHAPTER 16

"So I'm going to need a guest list from each of you, preferably within the next two weeks, as well as your preferred theme," Sydney said. Her sisters-in-law stared at her like she'd lost her mind. Maybe she had.

"Peaches, you don't have to do a different theme for each one of us," Jessamine said.

"But you're having a combined shower, that's no fun. This way it will be slightly personalized," Sydney said. They gave her the look again, the *Peaches has totally flipped her lid this time,* stare. Beside her, Chrissy shifted uncomfortably. Chrissy was her ringer, her comfort item. If she was doing this, and it was apparent she was, then at least she had her security Chrissy for support.

"I think it sounds like a marvelous idea," Marie said. "And of course I can do the food."

"Actually, Marie, I thought I would give you a break and let you enjoy the day. I'm having it catered."

"Catered?" Marie said, one eyebrow quirked. To her left, Vivian and Lou exchanged a look. *Wow,* Lou mouthed.

"It would be a nice way to support local businesses, I think," Sydney said.

Chrissy leaned close to whisper. "This is your version of self-harm."

Sydney elbowed her.

"Of course we can have it here," Marie interjected.

"Actually, I've rented a place."

"You…rented," Marie said, as if she didn't understand the words.

"It's going to be a large event. Lou will have the people from her company, Jess will have the people from TV, Vivian has friends from school, y'all have family, plus the Samperi family. We need space." What she needed was a buffer from her overbearing mother-in-law. If she had it at the Samperi homestead, Marie would take over, as she was now trying to do. If Sydney was really doing this, she was doing it on her own terms.

"I don't think…" Marie began, but Lou preempted her.

"I want a pony," she declared. It was her way to blurt inappropriate things to try and lighten the tension.

Sydney smiled. "Well, that sounds mighty fine, Lou, but you're going to be pretty far along then. I might suggest a burro instead."

Vivian snickered and Lou stared at her, wide-eyed with shock. Sydney was usually the type to go along with everything with a smile. "Oh, I like Peaches 2.0. I like her very much," Lou said.

"Kindergarten is going to be something different this year," Vivian agreed.

"Maybe I'll quit," Sydney blurted. She thought she meant it as a joke, but it ended on a serious note. When she first began teaching, it had felt like a calling. She was going to reach the kid she had been, the little girl who had no one else. She was going to change the world, be the light of her students' lives. She was that teacher who gave hugs to each student every day, in case it was the only one he or she had. She spent a small fortune buying food for the kids who had no food, clothes for the kids who had no clothes. But all of her efforts felt like throwing gravity at a black hole. Last year four of her kids were in foster care for a while before being put back with their abusive, neglectful parents. As a mandated reporter of child abuse, Sydney had called Children's Services three different times for two different children. Nothing happened, nothing whatsoever. Two of her students were homeless, drifting from couch to couch. Their little eyes were sad, hungry, desperate, and seemingly nothing Sydney did could reach them. The job that had once provided an escape was now another weight on her weary soul.

The room was silent and they were all giving the look again, even Chrissy this time. *Peaches 2.0 is cray-cray.* She forced a smile. "Any questions?"

Lou raised her hand.

"Yes, Lou? Would you like us to go before you and toss some palm fronds in front of the burro?"

Vivian snickered.

Lou pretended to consider. "Maybe. But I was actually channeling my husband just then. Should we say no gifts? I mean, all of us are basically bajillionaires. Is it right to have people bring us things?"

Sydney pressed a finger to her dimple, thinking. "It's less about people bringing you things and more about people desiring to help you celebrate. And I think we all know a lot of friends and loved ones who will contribute homemade items. But you do raise a good point. Why don't you talk to Benny and see what appropriate charitable contribution we could set up, for those who would rather donate than bring a gift? And we could match whatever is raised, of course."

Lou nodded, satisfied, and the meeting was adjourned.

"That was fun," Sydney said to Chrissy, surprised to realize she meant it. Taking the reins of her life was having a profound effect on her. She felt stronger, energetic, more resilient. This was the worst life could possibly throw at her, and she was surviving.

"Like a root canal," Chrissy muttered, reaching for another cannoli. "How are you not five hundred pounds?" She motioned to the table Marie had arranged, set with various charcuterie, grissini, biscotti, shrimp cocktail, and cannoli.

"I was on my way," Sydney said. She had lost ten pounds and felt much more like her old self than she had for a while.

"Oh, please," Chrissy muttered. "You're like Infertile Barbie."

Sydney snorted an indelicate laugh and covered her mouth.

"Maybe I should dye my hair pink." She touched the ends of her long, blond hair.

"No," Chrissy said.

"Why not? I thought you'd be all for it."

"I might be, if I thought you were sincere. But this is some kind of breakdown thing you'll regret the minute you do it, and then you'll either have to wait a year for it to grow out or you'll try to dye it back to blond and it will turn into straw."

"How do you know?"

Chrissy pointed to her own shorn head. "How do you think I ended up with this haircut? I tried to dye it silver. Turns out you should not do a walk-in appointment at a salon named The Scissor Shack and ask an eighty year old hairdresser named Doris for a trendy dye job."

"Duly noted," Sydney said. "Maybe I should pierce something."

"No," Chrissy said.

"Tattoo."

"Absolutely not."

Sydney huffed. "What can I do? I'm ready for something fun, some kind of adventure."

"Make a bucket list of actual adventures and we'll work on checking them off," Chrissy said. She reached for the entire shrimp cocktail and slid it into her lap. Bypassing all utensils, she dipped the shrimp in the liquid and ate them one by one.

At least Mama won't have leftovers, Sydney noted absently. Out loud she said, "Would you parachute with me?"

"Yep."

"Bungee jump?"

"Absolutely."

"Take hip-hop dance lessons?" Sydney tried.

Chrissy paused. "As long as there's no recital."

"Run a marathon?"

"What was your name again?" Chrissy asked, using a shrimp tail to scoop a giant glob of cocktail sauce into her mouth. She swallowed, wiped her crimson cocktail sauce fingers on a white cloth napkin, and spoke again. "There's another thing you need to do."

"What?"

"Something Lou said."

"A pony? Joe doesn't like horses."

"No, not a pony. Charity. You need to get involved. You're missing a piece of you, if you're not giving."

Sydney wrinkled her nose. "I did that scene, remember?" She gave a shudder, recalling all the charity boards she'd tried to sit on. It had been exactly like high school, trying to follow all the rules, to fit in with women pre-disposed to judge and dislike her. The happiest day of her life was when she finally gave it up and stopped trying to fit a prescribed mold that didn't fit.

"I'm not talking about committees with other rich women where nothing gets accomplished besides gossip and clique formations," Chrissy said.

"It's like you've sat in on one of the meetings," Sydney said.

"I did, remember? You dragged me along."

"Oh, right," Sydney said, smiling over the memory. Chrissy had been her weathervane. If she took her to a meeting and the women heartily accepted her, she would stay and continue to serve. Absolutely no one had accepted her, and Sydney had quit every committee. Everyone chalked it up to her continued breakdown, but for Sydney, it had been the opposite. She hated the committees, couldn't stand the people. Allowing herself to quit had been the first show of spirit, the tiniest spark of her true self to ever emerge in public.

"I think you need to get actually involved, in a hands-on way. You're loaded. Use your money for good. Give it away," Chrissy said. She finished the shrimp and reached for the charcuterie board.

"You know, I think you're right," Sydney said.

Chrissy shrugged her agreement and continued crunching a breadstick. Sydney reached for her phone. There was already someone in her life who needed a hand up. Now was the time to bestow it, whether her help was wanted or not.

CHAPTER 17

Sydney finished the cheer and realized the rest of her team wasn't with her. She turned to see Sherry and Alice, whispering together, darting furtive glances to her.

"Is there a problem?" she asked.

Sherry looked properly chastised, but Alice, who still wasn't over losing head cheerleader to Sydney, stepped forward. "Sherry was telling me the news about your sister, that she got pregnant from some guy in Lexington. I'm so sorry, Peaches. That must be difficult."

"She's managing just fine, thank you," Sydney replied, in a much sweeter tone than she wanted. In truth she had no idea how Belinda was doing because she was currently homeless and impossible to track down. And since she'd already had two abortions that Sydney knew of, it wasn't a stretch to say she would likely not get to meet this niece or nephew, either. A heavy weight of sadness latched around her neck, threatening to drag her under. She shook it off. She couldn't, wouldn't allow her family's mess to drag her down when she had finally found stability.

"I guess y'all are two peas in a pod," Alice continued.

Sydney pushed the hair off her forehead, feeling older than her seventeen years. Couldn't high school be over already so she and Joe could get on with their real lives? "Do I even want to know what you're talking about?"

"Come on, we've all seen the way your uniform's been clinging. You live with your boyfriend. Getting pregnant was an inevitability."

Sydney surveyed the expressions of her team and realized two things: Alice was lying. No one actually thought she was pregnant. But the intense curiosity and fascination on their faces told her they did all wonder what was going on with her and Joe. She could circumvent the nasty gossip and fortify them as allies if she told them everything right now, how Mrs. Samperi had bat ears, always on alert for the squeaky floorboard between her and Joe's rooms, that with four younger siblings around they had more chance of being alone together at school than they did at home, that she would never abuse the trust Joe's parents had placed in her, that Joe was too busy working fulltime after school to sneak around with her. That if her uniform was snug, which she doubted, it was only because she had regular access to food now and was eating full meals three times a day instead of sharing Joe's lunch with him every day as her only food source. Instead she laughed and waved her hand. "I guess you'll all know in nine months, one way or the other. Now can we get back to work? The sky looks like it's going to pour any minute."

Their glances darted to the sky, taking note of the gathering clouds, and they jumped to attention. Sydney worked them harder than usual, not as a punishment for their gossip but because if people were talking about her, which they clearly were, she wanted it to be for good things—how well she was doing as head cheerleader, how good her grades were, how nice she was to everyone she encountered.

She kept them working, even as the rain started, not letting them go until it turned from a spitting drizzle to a steady downpour. Laughing, they raced to their cars. Sydney didn't hurry. What was the point? She was walking home today. She would be soaked either way. She could call Mrs. Samperi to come get her, but she didn't want to disturb her when she was busy preparing dinner. And Sydney didn't mind the rain, loved it, in fact.

The rain was loud, but somehow she heard a familiar click beside her and swiveled to see Joe, camera in hand, snapping away. "What are you doing here?"

"I came to get my girl." He put away his camera and flicked open an oversized umbrella, grasping her hand to pull her beneath it. She stood on her toes to kiss him, inhaling the familiar scent of drywall dust that clung to his hair. Every day during nice weather he left school right after the last bell, gathered Benny, and headed to work with their dad, usually for five or six hours. Then he came home and did his homework (rather Sydney did his homework while he put up a token protest) and fell into bed exhausted, only to do it all over again the day after that. His break wouldn't arrive until the weather became too bad or too cold to work, and yet he had never complained, not once, not even in secret to her. If he could do all that and keep up a good attitude, Sydney could deal with a little mean-spirited gossip.

"How'd you get away?" she asked. It was cozy and intimate under the umbrella. Even though she was soaked to the skin and shivering, she was in no hurry to move. Sometimes life with Joe felt like a small series of perfect moments, as if she were living in a movie being scripted especially for her.

"Rain," he said.

"I love the rain," she said, standing on her toes to kiss him again.

He picked her up, securing her legs around his waist for easier access. "Me, too."

Laughter beside them caught their attention and they turned to look at the group of boys ogling them from under the bleachers.

"What's their deal?" Joe asked.

"That's where they go to smoke pot," Sydney informed him, amused. He was so far removed from the high school scene. Except for the fact that he actually attended high school and occasionally found the time to hang out with their group, it was like dating a grown man, one who worked nearly fulltime and felt the weight of family responsibility. He even looked like a grown man, a head taller than everyone else with broad shoulders and impressive muscles. Their football coach had begged, actually begged Mrs. Samperi to allow Joe to play. She felt so bad for refusing him so many times that she sent him a tray of biscotti to make up for it. Sydney had been the one to deliver it, and the coach had sighed.

"Some day that boy's going to regret being worked so hard."

His words had given Sydney pause. Would Joe have regrets? And would she factor into them?

"Where'd you go?" Joe asked her now, drawing her back to the present.

"Are you going to be sad someday that you're missing so much of the high school experience?" she asked.

He motioned to the bleachers beside them. "That high school experience? Plus, I'm dating our head cheerleader and homecoming queen. I think I have the high school experience all wrapped up." He tightened his arms on her and kissed her cheek.

"You're sweet," Sydney replied, kissing his cheek in return.

Thunder rumbled and he set her down. "I suppose we should get away from the metal bleachers before we get electrocuted. Do you think the tokers are smart enough to clear out, or should I go round them up?"

They paused to look and saw the group of boys slowly begin to empty out of their hiding spot. Joe squinted. "Is that an Eliopoulos? I didn't know they had a boy."

"He's the only one, I think. Last year his sister Amara was in my pre-calc class. She'd have a fit if she knew where he was right now."

Joe frowned. "I better never hear of any of our little brothers or sister under the bleachers."

"Of course they won't ever do that," Sydney said with assurance. "Our babies know better."

He squeezed her hand. "That's why you're their favorite, because you wrongly believe they're angels."

"They are angels, at least comparatively," she said sadly, reminded once again of her sister.

"I heard about Belinda," Joe said companionably, giving her hand another squeeze. "One of the guys on our crew today told me."

She sighed. "She's such a mess, Joey. And, selfish as it is, I can't help think that would be me without you."

"Nope, that would never be you, Peaches. You weren't on that trajectory when we met. You would be exactly as you are now, only sad and alone because of course you could never love anyone but me, even if your heart didn't know why."

"And where would you be, Joey? If you never moved to Kentucky, if we never met?"

They reached the car. He held the door for her, collapsed the umbrella, tossed it in the back, and sprinted to his side, waiting to answer until the door was closed. It was cozy and intimate in the car, the storm pounding on the roof, cocooning them in their own little world.

"Peaches, I really don't know, and it makes me sick to think of it. I would be a whole different person. My trajectory was *not* good, little punk boosting caps, trying everything to impress my friends. So if you think one of us has been changed for the better by this relationship, it's definitely me."

He eased his arm around her, pulling her close against his side. She rested her head on his shoulder. They sat in easy silence.

"I love the rain," she whispered.

"I know you do," he whispered.

"I keep being fooled into believing life can't possibly get any better, and then it does," she said.

"Think how much better it's going to be when high school is over and we're finally married."

Her stomach fluttered, picturing them as real grownups, a house full of kids. "I can't hardly wait."

"Me, neither. It's all downhill from here."

CHAPTER 18

"Peaches, is that you?"

Sydney's heart sank. She knew that voice. If only she were still running, she could keep pace and pretend not to hear. But she was finished with her run and doing her post-run walk, slow enough to converse. *Drat.*

"Hey, Alice." She kept the treadmill moving, in case her former schoolmate might take the hint and move along after the hello. No such luck. Beaming, Alice nabbed the treadmill beside her and hopped on.

"Hey, girl, what are you up to these days?"

"I'm still teaching kindergarten. What about you?"

"Ugh, mom stuff. I'll tell you what, these kids are wearing me out. You think the baby years are tough, but they're nothing compared to the tween years. I spend half my life in my minivan, being a chauffer."

"Hmm," Sydney replied, hoping the noise sounded sympathetic and not annoyed.

"How's Joe?" Alice asked.

"He's good. Busy."

"I'll bet. We all think it's so great, the fame the Samperis have brought to this community. It's so fun to see those home and garden channel cameras set up everywhere, and then to see our local celebrities on so many shows and magazines." She paused. "I've been surprised, actually, not to see your face more often. Seems like the kind of thing you'd enjoy, all that fame."

"Does it?" Sydney replied. By the time fourth grade rolled around, Sydney had figured out Alice's brand of meanness and learned how to master it, by being as vague as humanly possible while not letting her extreme irritation show.

"Of course I know you've had some hard years, and I'm awfully sorry about that." She paused, as if hoping Sydney might detail her painful years of deep depression and grief.

Keep waiting, Alice.

"But it's good to see you getting back out and about again, and getting in shape, too. Good for you." She did a full body scan of Sydney, noting with satisfaction the changes that had taken place since they were both size four cheerleaders. Sydney turned and did a full body scan of her in return. If Sydney had added twenty pounds since high school, Alice had added at least forty.

"Of course I need to get back in shape, too. It's why I'm here. But it's so hard when you have kids. Pregnancy does a number on the body, and then you lose so much sleep. And I am telling you, teenagers are as hard as everyone says they are. Girls today are so mean I can't believe it. It's unfathomable some of the things these girls say to my Kylee. I don't remember us being that mean when we were her age."

Sydney had to put out a hand to keep from flying off the treadmill in shock. Her mind flashed back to the note Alice had sent her in fifth grade. *Are you white trash, yes or no,* with the yes pre-circled. After that her barbs had become more sophisticated, but no less mean and hurtful. And the years had not changed her, if the words that came out of her mouth next were any indication.

"You are so lucky you can't have kids. I mean, seriously. I love mine, but I have no time for me anymore, no time for Adam. It's all about being a mom, that becomes your total identity. I really envy your freedom to do things like this whenever you want, to spend uninterrupted time with Joe. Some days I'd give anything to go back to that. But then I guess someone's going to have to pick the good nursing home for us someday, you know?" She chuckled at her joke, tossing Sydney a smile as if that should lessen the barb. Or maybe increase it. Who knew with Alice?

What would Peaches 2.0 do? A series of takedowns ran through Sydney's brain. She knew Alice well enough to craft something that could devastate her. Or there was option two: take the high road, smile pleasantly and pretend not to wounded. But suddenly a new option presented itself: stop pretending not to be wounded and choose to not actually be wounded. Other people said things to her all the time, usually in ignorance. Their words hurt terribly, but why did she let them? The words could only have us much power as she gave them, so why did she give them so much ability to wound and cause damage? She was Peaches Samperi, and she was fine. No one's ignorant, rude, or mean words could possibly take away all the things she now held dear, her hard-earned self-worth chief among them. She stopped the treadmill and reached for her towel.

"Yep," she said in a friendly tone. "Have a good day, Alice. Tell Adam we said hey." She wiped down the treadmill and walked away with a smile that must have looked as genuine as it felt if Alice's sour expression was any indication. For whatever reason, Sydney's happiness had always made Alice feel worse. Today she seemed to be feeling abysmal, meaning Sydney must truly be happy. *I am,* she thought. Despite everything, she had a new little light inside that refused to be extinguished and started to hum.

This little light of mine, I'm gonna let it shine...

CHAPTER 19

"*A*lone again, naturally," Sydney muttered, twirling her pen absently. Friday night, her sixth week of school at Duke, and absolutely everyone was at a party, including her roommate, Megan. Sydney had tried to go out, she really had. She had tried to do the high school thing and immerse herself in the social scene as she had then. But unlike then she had no Joe to protect her. Last week's party had ended with two drunk frat guys pinning her to the ground by her arms while a third tried to pour beer down her throat with a funnel. They had been laughing hysterically, oblivious to Sydney's panic and tears. It had felt like she was being water boarded as the beer clogged her throat, choking her. If that security guard hadn't showed up when he did, she had no idea what might have happened. As it was, he pulled her off the floor and drove her back to her dorm with a lecture about responsible partying behavior. The guys hadn't gotten a reprimand and she was the one who got taken home like a toddler and chastised. The unfairness weighed heavily, but her relief won out, so much that she thanked the man before dashing up the stairs and locking herself in her room.

Her classes were going great. She might be the only freshman who showed up for morning classes and had all A's. As for college life, she hated it as much as she thought she would. It was like being back home, her pre-Samperi home. Too much illicit activity; not enough structure or sleep. *Six weeks down, four years to go,* she thought sadly.

Someone knocked on her door. She blew out a breath, deciding to ignore it. A few people had sought her out, as if unable to believe she was actually staying home by choice. It was nice, she supposed, that they were being friendly. But she had no desire to party, zero desire to get wasted, and even less desire to do the next morning's walk of shame from a strange boy's room. What she wanted most was Joe. This was the longest they had ever been apart and she missed him the way one might miss an appendage.

The knock came again, louder and more insistent this time. She stood and yanked open the door, ready to tell whoever it was to go away, albeit politely, and instead came face to face with the person she'd just been thinking about.

"Joe," she blurted, reaching out a finger to poke his shoulder and make sure he was real.

"Ma thought you might not be eating proper. She sent a lasagna."

She saw now his hands were loaded with a massive lasagna, enough to feed her entire floor of men and women. She laughed, but it ended on a sob. Joe stepped inside, set the lasagna on her desk, and picked her up, holding her close.

"I missed you so much," he breathed. She could only nod. If she opened her mouth, it would all come flooding out, her misery, her fear, her certainty she was in the wrong place. He carried her to the bed, set her down, and stretched out beside her, all without letting her go. She clung harder and then, realizing they had precious and unusual alone time, pulled back to pelt him with kisses. He kissed her in return, his hands smoothing the length of her.

"I keep expecting Moss to run in and jump between us," she said. His youngest brother was their near constant companion, always inserting himself between them when they sat on the couch. Lucky for him he was adorable and Sydney loved him to pieces, as did Joe.

"Nope, I'm solo today," Joe said, his lips brushing against hers.

"How'd you manage that?" she asked, smoothing her hand over his hair. She felt like a part of her that had been turned off was now on and fully functioning and she couldn't stop smiling.

"I told Ma I was coming to bring you home," he said.

She blinked at him. "What?"

"I started listening to everything you didn't say. You hate it here. You're miserable. You didn't want to come."

"No, I..." she looked around the dreaded dorm room, loathing every square inch. "Oh."

"Peaches, I'm sorry."

She blinked at him. "For what?"

"For assuming this was what you should do because I thought it best, for trying to put you somewhere you didn't fit, for not listening. For all the things."

"You meant well, you all did. And I so badly wanted to make everybody proud. I mean, it's a really good school."

"UK is a good school, too, and you could live at home where you belong. Everybody's been sad and depressed without you, not just me. And we are proud of you, so proud. You have no idea. You're the only Samperi to go to college so far. That's huge."

"Is it really okay if I come home?"

"It's a necessity, unless your roommate is okay with me living under your bed. Turns out I can't actually survive without you," he said. "Now, where were we?"

"I think we were alone for the first time in our lives," she said.

He smiled. "Excellent." He reached for her, and the door burst open. They fully expected to see his four siblings tumble into the room as usual, but instead it was her roommate and another friend.

"Hey, Sister Sydney found a man and, hello hotness," the friend said as she plopped on the end of Sydney's bed.

"This is Joe," Sydney said, sitting up and latching on to his neck.

"Oh, the overblown attachment begins to make more sense," her roommate, said.

"This is my roommate, Megan, and her friend, Halley."

"Hi," Joe said, charming them in an instant with a swoon-worthy smile. With his height, muscles, broad shoulders, and crooked nose, he looked like a brute or, at the very least, a hockey player. But then he would bestow one of his signature shy smiles and all women in a ten-foot vicinity would lose their hearts forever.

Megan poked Sydney. "You said he was adorable. I was picturing a baby koala or something. This is like hot quarterback."

"I'm the baby koala," Sydney said, clinging to Joe's neck.

"And my mom wouldn't let me play football," Joe added, making them laugh, even though he was serious.

"We're going to another party," Halley added. "You guys want to join in?"

Joe surveyed Sydney. "What do you think, Peaches? One last hurrah?"

With him there, it would be fun; with him there, she would feel safe. "Absolutely." She kissed his cheek, slid off the bed, and spent the evening saying farewell to Duke.

CHAPTER 20

"Thanks for agreeing to have lunch with me," Sydney said, giving her guest a wide smile.

"Thanks for asking me to go," her niece, Justice, said.

"Fifteen dollars for a burger, geez. Fancy schmancy, Syd," her sister, Belinda, inserted.

Sydney had only invited her niece but, as their mother before them, Belinda was possessive about what she felt was hers, Justice included. Over the years she had thwarted Sydney's best attempts to give Justice a leg up, making fun of her for buying books and savings bonds instead of toys. Sydney had circumvented her to pay her school fees and always slipped her money or clothes whenever they happened to meet which, to Sydney's dismay, seemed to grow fewer and farther between as her niece aged. She had thought her niece would choose to spend more time with her as she matured, would see the chaos of her home life and compare it to the calm Sydney offered. Instead she had joined a rowdy group of friends and her life was becoming a repeat of her mother's.

"How was your birthday?" Sydney asked Justice. Ignoring her sister's bile and drama was always the better route.

"Good, really good. Thank you for the check. I used it to buy some boots and new makeup." She bit her lip, probably worried Sydney would think it was too frivolous. Sydney didn't, however. She had been fifteen once.

"Excellent," she said, smiling.

"Know what Syd got for her fifteenth birthday?" Belinda interjected. "Diamond earrings. You can guess who those were from."

"Uncle Joe bought you diamonds when you were fifteen?" Justice said, awed. If there was one thing she thought was amazing about Sydney's life, it was her relationship with Joe. Being rescued by a boy and finding lifelong love at twelve were what dreams were made of to a struggling teenage girl.

"No, his parents did," Sydney said. It was the first thing of value she had ever owned in her life. She used to open the box and stare and stare and stare at the earrings. "I can't believe you remember that," she added to her sister.

Belinda shrugged. "I remember you wouldn't keep them at our house, too afraid one of us would steal them."

Sydney shrugged. One of them would have stolen them, but she wasn't in the mood to argue or insult, and especially not in front of her niece. "So, Justice, I wanted to talk to you about something."

"Here we go," Belinda said, closing her menu. "She's not coming to live with you, she's happy at home."

"That's not what I was going to say," Sydney said, stung. She had offered before, when Belinda was still in her downward spiral. There had been a string of men and, finally after what seemed to be rock bottom, she met a semi-nice guy and began to get her life in order. For the last few years, she had been stable, if not thriving. At least she hadn't been arrested, at least they had been living in the same place for a few years, not couch hopping with friends, as she had done when Justice was little. She took a breath and pushed away her irritation, focusing on her niece once again. "Joe and I would like to pay for your college."

Justice blinked at her. "College?"

"Yes, college. The college of your choice, whichever one you choose. The only stipulation is that you attend regularly and keep your grades up."

"What if I want to go to Harvard?" Justice asked. Beside her, Belinda snorted her derision.

"Then we'll pay for Harvard," Sydney said without hesitation.

"What if I want to go to community college?" Justice tried.

"Then we'll pay for that, too."

"And a car?" Justice tried.

You are your mother's daughter, Sydney thought, but she hadn't grown up in the same family for nothing. "If you make it through two years of college, declare a major with intent to graduate, and make all A's, we'll buy you a brand new car." Justice licked her lips and swallowed.

"I'll think about it."

Sydney nodded, unwilling to push.

"You know I have three other kids," Belinda added resentfully.

"And when they get to be this age, we'll have the same conversation," Sydney said. She meant it, but it was unlikely to ever progress past a conversation. Unless something drastically changed, her younger niece and nephews were on track to follow their fathers into lives of chaos and crime.

"Well, then, I guess this is probably a poor time to tell you," Belinda said, smiling in triumph.

"Tell me what?" Sydney asked, heart filling with dread. Any time her sister got that look, it usually ended in pain for Sydney.

"Mom," Justice implored.

Belinda ignored her and hastened on. "Justice is pregnant."

Sydney blinked at her niece who squirmed miserably. "Oh," Sydney said. Inside she withered. Even this child could get pregnant as easily as breathing. She let out a breath. It really wasn't about her or her problems right now. She saw the fear and sadness on Justice's face and her heart melted. "What are you going to do, Justice?"

"I don't know," Justice said in a small voice, tears now making a white trail down her overly made up face. Sydney pushed away from the table, moved closer, and gathered her up in a crushing hug. Justice wept on her shoulder, bawling like her kindergarteners when they skinned their knees.

Belinda grunted in disgust. "I'm going to the bathroom. Y'all pull yourselves together. This is embarrassin'." She pushed away from the table and stormed off. Sydney rubbed Justice's back, patting until her sobs came to an end. They separated. Justice mopped her face with the napkin and darted a hasty look toward the bathroom.

"I want you to have it," she whispered.

Sydney froze. "What?"

"The baby. I want you to take it. You can raise it. I know how much you and Uncle Joe want kids."

Sydney's heart somersaulted with joy. It was the perfect solution. Outwardly, her face remained impassive. "That's a very big, mature decision, sweetheart. You need to take a long time to think about it, to weigh what's best for you and the baby before you make any life-altering decisions. Will you do that for me? Will you give it serious consideration? And talk to the baby's father about it, too, okay?" Justice nodded and sniffled. Sydney patted her hand. Belinda returned and they tried to resurrect the lunch, talking about whatever innocuous topic they could find. But Sydney's mind was already rushing ahead, joyfully attaching itself to the vision of herself with her niece's baby. *I might be a mom after all,* she thought, making a conscious effort not to get too excited.

CHAPTER 21

"Christmas, Christmas, Christmas, Christmas." Sydney danced Moss around the grand entryway, pirouetting him round and round while he laughed.

"My turn, Peaches, I need to learn to lead," he said, reaching for her other hand and attempting to spin her in return. Sydney laughed, ducking low under their combined arms each time he spun. "Guess what, I have a new girlfriend."

"Moss, you lady killer," Sydney said. She let go of his hand, picked him up, and began spinning him in earnest while he giggled incessantly.

"Hey," Joe said, startling her. His presence filled the doorway. Sydney took a stumbling step and nearly fell over, clutching Moss tighter so he didn't tumble from her grasp. Joe reached out and righted them both, leaning in to muss Moss's hair and kiss his cheek. He was always that kid, with curly locks that begged to be tousled and cherubic pink cheeks that begged to be kissed. Sydney followed suit, adding her fingers to his curls before kissing his other cheek and setting him down.

"Got a new girlfriend, Joe," Moss announced proudly, eight-year-old chest puffing.

"What for, Moss? You only ever need one," Joe said, picking Sydney up and tossing her over his shoulder like a sack of potatoes while she giggled.

"Well, that's because there's only one Peaches," Moss said sincerely. He kissed his finger and touched it to Sydney's calf before running off to play.

"Geez, that kid," Joe said. "Smoother than I ever was."

"Or ever will be," Sydney added, giggling harder when he bounced her up and down and smacked her bottom. He set her down and kissed her. "Come out with me tonight."

"Okay," she agreed.

"What? You don't have to study or write a paper or read some boring textbook?" He pressed his palm to her forehead, checking for a fever.

"No, because guess what, it's Christmas break, Joey." She clutched his shirt and bounced up and down, dancing with excitement. Christmas at her house had always been a time of dread. It meant her parents would be home longer with more time to drink. It meant she would be away from school, away from Joe. It meant the comparison between her family and everyone else's would be more stark as Sydney and her sister spent Christmas day scrounging for food, trying not to think about the ham everyone else in the world was likely eating that day. The Samperis did Christmas up right. Every square inch of their lavish house was decorated and lit and the food, oh, the food. Mrs. Samperi went all out, started baking and freezing things weeks ahead of time in preparation. It was like living in a movie, in an honest to goodness movie, to say nothing of the presents, which still made Sydney uncomfortable. She was happy without them, happier, actually. All she needed was this family; the material possessions meant nothing to her.

"I have a confession," Joe said.

"What?" she asked, standing on her toes to be nearer him. Six years and she still couldn't get enough. She would never, ever get enough of Joseph Samperi.

"Every time I see you like that with Moss, I get a little teary," he whispered.

"What? Why?" she asked, concerned.

"Because I picture you like that with our kids, and my heart can't take it. You're going to be the best mom ever, Peaches, because you have all the love in the world in your big, sweet heart." He kissed her, and now it was Sydney's turn to be a little teary.

"That's only 'cause I've been so well loved by you," she returned, easing her arms around him and pressing closer.

He gave her a squeeze. "Go get dressed."

"What should I wear?"

He rolled his eyes. "As if I would know. In fact, I'd be perfectly happy if you wore nothing at all."

"You're so altruistic that way, Mr. Samperi."

"I'm a giver by nature," he said, kissing her.

She broke away and took a step back. At this rate she'd never get changed. "I'm going to let Jess pick my outfit. Your sister's developing quite the flair for fashion."

"No, she's not. She's a baby forever," Joe said.

"They're gonna grow up, Joe. Gotta let 'em go sometime."

He stuck out his lip in a sincere-looking pout, full sadness now. One of the things she loved best about Joe, and there were many to choose from, was how much he loved his brothers and sister. "It's okay, I'll make you some replacements," she said, touching her finger to his protruding lip.

He wagged his brows at her and, giggling, she turned to dart up the stairs.

Forty five minutes later she returned, wearing a dress Jessamine helped her pick out. Her hair had similarly been styled by Joe's thirteen-year-old sister, but Sydney did her own makeup because Jessamine wasn't allowed to wear it yet, though she did in secret and was quite good at the application. She had wanted to do Sydney's face, but, knowing Joe's mother, she would have guessed the truth, that Jessamine was so good at it because she practiced on herself. No need to get the budding teenager grounded in order to further her own night out.

Joe stood at the bottom of the stairs wearing his good jeans and a gray sweater that pulled taut on his impressive pecs. Sydney felt like it was prom all over again, or maybe a little bit more as he stared up at her, awed. It was almost that time, time for them to get engaged, and it was almost Christmas. He had to have something up his sleeve, if not now, soon.

"Wow, you clean up good," he said, eyes raking over her in a way that made her blush.

"Too much?" she asked, indicating the dress with a flourish.

"Well, I'd always like to see you in something less," he said.

Sydney's flush deepened to a blush and she put her finger to her mouth, looking around for his mother. It was normally the sort of comment which, if overheard, would end with him being smacked with a wooden spoon on whichever part of him Marie could reach. Joe held out his hand to her. She took it. He wove their fingers together and led her out the door. Her heart was thudding. *This is it,* she thought. *Tonight I'm going to get engaged.*

Joe said nothing as he tucked her in the car and started to drive. They ambled for a while and ended up at their high school hangout, the local pizza parlor. Sydney darted him a curious look. He said nothing, kept his gaze fastened away from her. She pressed her lips together, trying to stop a smile. *He doesn't want me to see his eyes because I'll know,* she thought.

They walked into the pizza parlor, hand in hand, and their usual table in the back erupted in cheers.

"Surprise," Joe said, giving her hand a squeeze. All their old gang was there, all their friends from high school, whom Sydney hadn't seen in months. She could only hope her face didn't show how little she had missed them.

"Peaches!" Cassius Carter erupted from his booth and picked her up in a crushing hug. "Oh, wow, you look so good. College agrees with you."

"Easy there, Cassius, or Joe's going to start flexing," Sherry Wentworth said. Sydney always thought she had a thing for Cassius, who had never seemed too interested in her.

"Hey, Cassius, hey, Sherry," Sydney said, absently patting Cassius's back as he let her go. "How're y'all? Cassius, how's officer training?"

"I haven't killed anyone yet, so," he held up double crossed fingers, smiling when she laughed.

"Well, keep up the good work, I guess." Joe was across the room talking and laughing with Savannah Morgan, and Sydney had to tamp down her hackles. Savannah had always had a thing for him, Sydney knew. It was one of the reasons she was such a shrew all through cheerleading. To see them talking and laughing like old friends now was an unpleasant reminder of old high school rivalries. Why had Joe brought her here? Why had he arranged a get together with these people? He knew she didn't actually like them, couldn't care less if she never saw them again. As far as she was concerned, he and his family were the only people she needed or wanted in her world. Did he not know that? Did he not know *her*?

After Duke, he had made a concerted effort to listen to not only what she said, but what she didn't say, to parse through the subtext and get to the real Sydney. She had never felt more loved than she had since her return from North Carolina a few weeks ago. Until tonight when he brought her to a room full of people who meant nothing to her. And it wasn't that he had brought her here. Of course she would be willing to get together with them, if that was what he wanted. It was that he presented it as if it were some sort of gift to her. *Surprise, I arranged to spend an entire evening with people you don't actually like. Are you happy, sweetheart?*

Then again, it was entirely possible she was reading too much into it, as she was apt to do. She had put too much on this evening, she realized. Just because she thought it was time for them to become officially engaged didn't mean Joe did. She took a breath and made her way around the room, stopping to have a polite chat with each person, even Savannah, the cow.

She and Joe didn't get a chance to talk the whole night, so busy were they catching up with their old crowd. Sydney hesitated to call them friends. The boys she'd liked, but the girls she hadn't trusted as far as she could throw. They had constantly plied her for secrets about her and Joe. Sydney had never told them any, not wanting to give them ammunition on the strange battlefield girls face in high school. Knowledge was power, and Sydney was glad to realize these people had little power over her life. Most of them had forgotten what her family was like, if they ever knew. Sydney had been careful to be perfect, so perfect in how she presented herself. Perfect hair, perfect makeup, perfect clothes, perfect figure, perfect nails, perfect grades, perfect extracurriculars, perfect manners. Perfectly nice, perfectly calm, perfectly arranged. She had somehow spent her entire high school career without messing up once, had become head cheerleader, homecoming queen, and prom princess with only Joe realizing the crushing weight of insecurity and sadness she was under. Was it any wonder she hadn't missed them? None of them knew her at all. She was a stranger to every one in this room except Joe, who strangely hadn't looked at her all night.

And when Savannah suggested they all move the party to the old cabin, the place everyone used to go to drink and party, Joe readily agreed without even consulting her.

"Did you have fun?" Joe asked, holding the door to his truck for her.

She gave him a nod and didn't speak. He jogged to his side of the truck and hopped inside. "You know, now that I've gained some objectivity, I can say for certain that Cassius has a thing for you and probably always has." He darted her a glance to check her response.

She shrugged. "I've never been interested in Cassius."

Joe faced forward, relieved.

"Although, if we're comparing crushes, Savannah's always had one on you. And, my, didn't you spend an awful long time talking to her tonight?"

His head swiveled to look at her. "Is that jealousy, Miss Parker? I didn't know you had it in you." He grinned.

She leaned over the seat and rested her hand on his thigh. "Just so you know, Joey, if I ever thought you would cheat on me, sugar bear, I'd destroy you."

He laughed out loud and took her hand, giving it a squeeze. "Good thing it won't ever happen then. Did you have fun? It was great to see everyone again, wasn't it?"

"Hmm," she replied, turning to gaze out the window. They were heading into the backwoods and she was totally turned around. Even though she'd lived here all her life, she rarely had any idea where she was. Directions had never been her strong suit, and Joe always drove and navigated. "I should start driving more. My skills are getting rusty."

"You drive to Lexington every day for school," he reminded her.

"Interstate is different than this," she said, motioning to the hills and trees around them.

"I would say the Interstate is more nerve wracking. I'd rather do this any day."

"That's 'cause you're a country boy at heart, and I'm a sophisticated city girl."

She didn't notice how quiet he got until he pulled off the road and parked. "Something wrong?" she asked when he came over to her door and lifted her out. He took her hand, a necessity in the middle of the woods, as they now were.

"It's just, Peaches, are you sure you want to be with me?"

She stopped short. "What are you saying, Joe? Why would you ask that?"

He tugged her hand, urging her along. "Sometimes I think we want different things. You love the city and adventure and action so much. And you're right, I am a country boy. I didn't go to college. This is it for me, this is all I'm ever going to be. I'm going to live here forever and work construction, the end. You could have so much more, could be so much more. You could go away and live somewhere grand."

In answer, she burst into tears. He stopped and wrapped his arms around her. "Why are you crying?"

"Because it sounds like you want to get rid of me."

"No, never ever. I'm giving you an out. It's kind of now or never, you know? Last chance to back out before it becomes official."

"It was always official for me." She peeled her head off his chest and looked up at him, squinting against the sudden glare of light. "What on earth?" she asked, shading her eyes against the unexpected brightness. She expected to see the glow of the old cabin. Instead she saw a Ferris wheel, in the middle of the field, lit up and waiting. She gasped and clutched at his shirt.

"It was always official for me, too, Peaches," he whispered. "C'mere." He took her hand again and led her forward, to the Ferris wheel. One of the doors was open. He settled her inside and the ride started.

"What?" she stuttered. "What? How?" When she looked at him, he held an open box in his hand, a massive diamond glittering in the glow from the ride.

"I wanted it to be a surprise," he said, voice thick. "Peaches, six and a half years ago, the most beautiful girl in the world said hey to me on what up to then was the worst, most miserable, loneliest day of my entire life. And everything changed, flipped upside down in an instant. No longer was Kentucky a dreaded place to be, it was home, full of promise and opportunity because she was there. She gave me my first peach and then, two years later on this very ride, in this very seat, gave me the best kiss of my life, my first kiss with her. I don't want anything in life but you, ever, for the rest of our lives. Will you do me the honor of making it officially official and marry me?"

She nodded, unable to speak, tears coursing down her cheeks. Smiling now, Joe slid the ring on her finger and kissed her. They kissed for a while and then he pulled away and settled his arm around her while the wheel continued to spin.

"So, the pizza parlor, that was all a ruse to throw me off track?" she said.

"Girl, are you kidding me? I know you can't stand those people. Though, I have to say, the way you work a room is something else, Sydney Parker. If teaching doesn't work out, you should definitely consider politics." He gave her shoulder a squeeze and kissed her cheek.

"Who's running the wheel?" she asked.

"Benny."

"How did you do this?" she asked. They were in the middle of an abandoned field. How could he possibly have gotten the wheel here, and where was the electricity coming from?

"Magic," he said. "It's the same kind of magic you bring to my life, Peaches. And I promise that as long as you'll let me, I'll keep providing the same for you."

"Forever and ever and ever," she murmured, feeling teary all over again.

"Amen," Joe said and kissed her.

CHAPTER 22

"Where's your guard girl?"

Sydney heard Cassius's voice and hid an internal wince. How did they always end up at the gym at the same time? Normally it wasn't a big deal because Chrissy was always in tow, until today.

"Tummy ache from too much shrimp scampi," Sydney replied. Whatever of Mama Samperi's bounty they couldn't manage to eat got passed on to Chrissy who was especially partial to seafood.

Cassius chuckled. "It happens to the best of us. Need a spotter?"

It was her bad luck she had been heading to the weight bench, intending to work the hand weights. But the fact was she would prefer the press, and what was the harm in spotting? "Sure, thanks."

She told him which weights to put on the bar and he did it for her, one eyebrow aloft. "Impressive," he said.

"Trying to stave off the osteoporosis," she said, and he laughed.

They were quiet while she lifted. Cassius challenged her to do a few more reps than usual and offered some suggestions on her form.

"Thanks," she said, sitting up to watch as he racked her weights and wiped down the bar.

"No problem."

"I'd offer to spot you, but you might actually die because I don't think we're on the same level yet."

"We've never been on the same level, Syd," Cassius said. He claimed the seat beside her, and they sat in comfortable silence a minute. Sydney knew she should get up and move away, but she was tired, and the silence was pleasant.

"What's up with you and the guard girl?" he asked after a bit.

"What do you mean?" Sydney asked.

"You're an unlikely pairing," he said.

"Not at all," she replied.

"Come on, Syd. You look like you fell out of a catalogue and she..."

"Hey, now, watch it," Sydney warned.

"Looks like appearances aren't important," he finished.

"They're not important to me, either."

He snorted a laugh. "Miss Homecoming Queen? You're the most put together girl I've ever known. I don't think I have ever once seen you with a hair out of place."

Her nose wrinkled in annoyance. "They're not. All I care about, the only thing, is someone's heart, whether it's pure and kind and loyal, and Chrissy's heart is all those things."

"Now that sounds like the Syd I know, have always known. We've been pals a long time, you know it? Thirty one years, by my calculation. I pre-date Joe. Now there's a thought, huh?" He nudged her with his elbow.

"That is odd. I don't actually remember time existing before Joe," she said, nudging him in return. "Can I ask you a question, serious and personal?"

"Shoot."

"Does having children make it harder to separate?"

"Oh, yeah," he said, nodding. "I'm tied to Sherry for life now, you know? There's nothing to bind two people together like having a baby or, in our case, three babies in rapid succession. I think that might be part of it, though. We lost ourselves somewhere in there, became parents instead of husband and wife." He blew out a breath.

"So you think if you hadn't had kids together, it would have been easy to leave?"

"Girl, you would have seen my dust trails from space. Sherry's insane." She laughed and shoved his shoulder. "I'm serious here. I know I was part of the problem, but the woman is nuttier than a fruitcake. Seriously, I'm keeping tabs on my kids for signs of genetic mental illness."

She clutched her stomach and bent over, laughing. "You stop that. That's no way to talk about the mother of your children."

"I suppose you're right, as usual. Sydney Samperi Kindness Camp, 101. But what are you asking me for? You know how it is after you become a parent."

She flinched. It was always impossible to her there were people in the world who might now know about their long, sad struggle. "No, Joe and I don't have kids."

"What? No way, of course you do," he said.

"I'm fairly certain I'd know. We're infertile."

"Oh, man, I'm sticking my foot in it all over the place. Sorry, Syd."

"It's okay. I mean, it's not, but not because of you. I'm trying to find my peace with it." She motioned to the weight bench. "By any means possible, I guess. Welcome to my mid-life crisis, pull up a chair."

He laughed. "Girl, if you're mid-life we're all in trouble. You look exactly like you did in high school, still the prettiest girl I've ever known in real life."

"Cassius," she said, shaking her head.

"What? That's fact, not flirting." He squinted. "I could swear you guys had kids. I saw you with a baby last year. Don't tell me you're those baby-stealing bandits we've been looking for."

"That was Moss's baby, Joe's youngest brother."

"Oh, right. I can't believe I forgot. I took that call, you know? The night she was attacked. I really thought his girlfriend was going to die."

"We all did," Sydney said, shuddering.

"How's she doing?"

"Good. They're married now. She's pregnant, actually."

"Ouch, does that hurt?"

"Yes, but I'm coming to terms with the fact that my sadness can't preclude someone else's happiness."

He shook his head. "Oh, Sydney, you're just too good."

"You can't know how much I wish that were true. I'm a sad mess, a total fraud who pretends to have it all together, but really I'm a walking nightmare."

"No," he said, shaking his head.

"Cassius, you want to know what my mother said to me on prom night?"

"What?"

"I was living with Joe's family then."

"Joe's always been the luckiest loser this side of the Mason-Dixon," Cassius inserted.

"Ha, he'd laugh if he heard you say that. The years we lived with his parents were our most chaste, by far. Hard to get alone time in an Italian family with four younger siblings. Anyway, it was prom and I had this crazy notion to stop by and see my parents. I wanted them to maybe take a picture, tell me I looked pretty. I guess for a minute I wanted the dream, parents who loved and supported me. So we pulled up in the limo Joe rented, walked to the door, and knocked. My mom yanked it open, scanned me up and down, and said, 'You can put a fancy dress on white trash, but it's still white trash.' And Joe took my hand and led me back to the car and we drove away. And that's the voice I have in my head, no matter where I go, no matter what I do."

"I absolutely refuse to believe that. Know why?"

She shook her head.

"'Cause I've known you thirty one years."

"You know the person you think I am. You don't know the real me."

"Try me. I made a study of you for many a year, Miss Sydney, watched you from afar, dreaming and hoping for the possibility that Joe Samperi might one day mess up and make room. I know where you came from, know how far you've come, and I know something else, too, something I bet not even you know."

"What?" she couldn't help but ask.

"I know you think it was Joe who got you here, but you're wrong. You would have turned out the same without him. It was in you all along, Syd, this will to survive and thrive, to be better than your upbringing, to work hard, to go to college, to be kind. That's what Joe saw when he looked at you, what those of us who really knew you understood. The magic is you."

Sydney wasn't certain how his words were intended, but as ever they had the effect of reminding her of Joe, of the magic he'd promised when they were long ago engaged. She missed those days of dreaming and believing the best was still to come. But, really, why shouldn't it be? What was stopping them from having an extraordinary life?

"Let's go have coffee. It sounds like you need a listening ear. We're friends, I can be a friend, no strings." He put his hands up in the "no touch" symbol.

Sydney gave him a smile and shook her head. "I'll have coffee with you if Chrissy comes along, or Joe."

"Are you scared of me, of little old Cassius?" he asked, aiming for innocence and failing mightily.

"No, but a good marriage requires good boundaries." She held up her hand to show him her ring. "Joe and I have always observed those, and always will."

"Do you have a good marriage?" Cassius asked.

Sydney stood and reached for her towel. "None of your business," she said and walked away.

CHAPTER 23

"Uhat do you want?" Joe asked for the fourth time, tone testy and impatient.

"I don't care," Sydney answered in the same tone.

"You care, I know you do, Just tell me."

She pressed her fingers to her temples. "Joe, I don't care. Whatever your mom wants is fine." It was their third disagreement of the morning, and it was taking place in front of his family. In their defense, it was hard to find a place to argue alone when they all lived together. One big happy Samperi family, plus Sydney, who was making things difficult by virtue of trying not to make things difficult. She was on the verge of tears, and she hated it.

"Excuse me," she said and fled the room. She ran up to her bedroom, quietly closed the door, and lay facedown on the bed to hide her tears. A minute later, someone tapped on her door. "I don't want to talk right now, Joe," she said, voice muffled by the quilt.

The door opened. "It's not Joe," his mother said, poking her head in like a turtle.

Sydney sat up and wiped her face. "Oh, hi. I'm sorry."

"Why?"

"Joe and I have been bickering all morning. I know it must be unpleasant."

Marie chuckled as she came in and perched on Sydney's bed. "Oh, honey, if Samperis got upset anytime there was a disagreement or a little yelling, we'd never get anything accomplished" She reached out and petted Sydney's head. Sydney leaned into the touch as if she were starving for it, which she was. Her mother had never touched her this way, not once in twenty years. "Do you want to talk about it?"

"Am I allowed to talk about it with you? You're his mom."

"Yes, and I love him, but sometimes girls have to stick together."

Unable to bear it any longer, Sydney pitched forward and pressed her face into the older woman's lap, weeping. "I don't even know. The closer it gets to the wedding, the more we fight. We've never fought before. I don't understand and I'm scared and I love him so much. Why is this happening?" Her words were such a garbled mess, she had no idea if they were understood. Perhaps that was why Marie took a minute to answer.

"I know why."

"Why?" Sydney asked with dread. Was Marie going to tell her they weren't meant to be? That they were too young? That they should postpone or, worse, cancel the wedding?

"It's because you're breathing."

Sydney sniffed and sat up. "What?"

"Honey, where did you ever get the idea that being together, that loving someone, means never hashing anything out? It's okay to discuss things, to bicker, to disagree, even to yell as long as you always come back together, which you will. We're human. We have bad days, we get annoyed. Marriage taps into all your baggage, it will test every insecurity, challenge every stronghold in your life. And that is perfectly normal. The trick is to always come back when the feelings burn away, to not hold on to resentments and let them fester. Clear the air like a powder keg if you want, but then apologize and move on." She rubbed a comforting circle on Sydney's back. "You're going to be okay."

Sydney nodded, somehow believing her. This time when someone knocked on her door, she knew it was Joe. "Can I come in?"

Sydney nodded again, too choked up to speak. "Ma, can I have a minute?"

"Be nice," his mother warned, jutting a finger in his face.

He rolled his eyes but tossed her a smile, closing the door behind her on her way out. He sat and scooped Sydney into his lap. "I'm sorry I was pressuring you. But this is our wedding, not my mom's."

"Your parents are paying for it," she reminded him.

"So? It's still our wedding. You're not being unreasonable by voicing your opinion. I don't want to marry my mom's puppet. I want to marry you, Peaches, with all your faults and foibles and secretly strong opinions you try to pretend don't exist. It bothers me, really bothers me, when you try to shrink up to nothing to make others like you. " He kissed her cheek. She relaxed and rested her head on his shoulder.

"I like the silver tuxes best," she said softly.

"Thank you," he said, giving her a squeeze. "Can you do one thing for me, pretty please?"

"What?"

"I know fighting is new for us and neither of us likes it. It's a lot more fun to be in gooey love all the time, but it's probably not very realistic. In the future, will you please stay and work it out? Go toe to toe with me, if you want. Yell, rail, throw stuff. Just don't disappear and run away and withdraw. It freaks me out when I can't reach you, when you close yourself off."

"When my parents fought, I used to go to my room and hide to be safe. I guess the habit got entrenched."

He was silent a minute, digesting that. "I'm used to my parents always yelling until they figured it out."

"We'll probably figure it out eventually," she said.

"Definitely," he agreed. He kissed her, and it didn't take long for them to forget why they'd been fighting to begin with.

CHAPTER 24

Sydney hadn't told Joe about Justice's baby. She didn't want to get his hopes up until something became certain. Though, in reality, the truth was that she had barely seen him in five days. Summers for him meant long days, from before sunup until after sundown. She told herself it was normal for them not to see each other much during his busy season, but a long time ago, back in the beginning, she used to take him supper or wait to eat until he got home. Now she grabbed something small and healthy in her newfound quest to get back in shape.

She stopped at her sister's house to try and touch base with Justice, who had been dodging her texts and calls. No way was she going to pressure her about the baby, the girl was only a baby herself. But she was worried about her, and she wanted to make certain she was getting proper prenatal care.

No one answered the first knock, but that wasn't so unusual. Inside the television blared, so she knew someone was home. She knocked a second and a third time and, eventually, Justice opened the door and stepped onto the porch. It was clear to Sydney she had been crying, for a long time if her puffy eyes were any indication.

"Honey, what is it? Is everything okay?" Her glance darted to the house, her ears straining for signs of stress or tension. She was suddenly reminded of that long ago day when Mrs. Samperi came for her, rescued her from her fighting parents. Her sister's boyfriend seemed like an okay guy, and she had never caught wind of any abuse from him. But she was ready to do a quick getaway with her niece, if needed.

Justice shook her head.

Sydney lowered her voice and stepped forward. "Are you okay? Are you safe?"

The door was ripped open and her sister towered in the doorway. "She's fine, quit asking her that. You make it sound like we beat her, which we don't. Stop being so high and mighty superior. We both know why you're here."

"I'm only here to check on Justice. I haven't heard from her in days. I wanted to make sure she was healthy and feeling okay."

Belinda looked at Justice. "Did you tell her?"

Justice shook her head, looking miserable, staring at the porch floor.

"Tell me what?"

"The baby's dad is eighteen. He was afraid he'd get arrested for statutory. He took her to get an abortion," Belinda blurted. Her voice was harsh, but Sydney could hear the underlying grief. She may not have wanted to be a grandmother before she turned forty, but she also hadn't wanted Justice to get rid of the baby. And inside Sydney a hollow chasm opened, an old wound re-pricked. No baby for her, no chance at being a mother. She wanted to cry from the unfairness of it, but Justice was still a little girl who had made a woman's decision and now must live with that decision so, once again, she pulled her niece into her embrace and gave her a tight comforting hug.

"Oh, honey," she murmured, holding Justice while she wept. Belinda closed the door and walked away, likely so she also wouldn't cry. Retreating from hurt was the one thing they had in common.

"I'm sorry, Aunt Syd. I'm sorry," Justice murmured over and over.

"I'm sorry for you," Sydney said and meant it. She pulled away and tipped her niece's face up. "If you want to talk to somebody, a counselor, a doctor, me, let me know, okay? This is too big for you to handle on your own. And, Justice."

Justice blinked at her with big eyes.

"I'd rethink the boyfriend. Any boy who treats you the way that boy treated you does not have your best interest at heart, likely does not love you."

Justice nodded, looking miserable. Sydney gave her one final hug and sent her back inside. Swallowing hard, she palmed her keys and walked back to the car. It always amazed her how much it could hurt to mourn for something that had never been. She mourned every month a baby that failed to arrive, and now she mourned this baby who, though it existed, had never been hers.

Tears ran unchecked down her cheeks the long ride home, but once she arrived there, she wiped them away. She sat in her car in the garage and stared into the darkness. *I will not give in to the grief,* she vowed. *I will not go back to that bed and that TV. I will not give up the gains I've made. I will make supper, and when Joe gets home, we will talk, really talk about the things that have been going on with us.*

Resolved, she wiped her face once more, fixed her mascara and lip gloss, and went inside the house.

When Joe arrived home two hours later, supper was made and ready to be served. She greeted him with a smile that soon died when she saw his expression. He stood in the doorway staring at her, pale and shaking.

"What happened?" she asked.

He didn't answer. She had never seen him like this, he looked like he was about to keel over. Had he somehow learned about Justice? Had he known how much Sydney wanted her baby and was afraid she would regress?

She wiped her hands and went forward. "Joe? Sweetheart, what's wrong? What is it?" She put out a hand, but he took a step back.

"I kissed my secretary."

She stared at him, the words not making sense. "What? No, of course you wouldn't do that."

"But I did," he whispered.

Sydney turned and fled. For once he didn't call her to come back.

"You're the most beautiful bride in the history of bridedom."

"Is bridedom a word?" Sydney asked.

"Sure," Joe said, holding her close, his eyes alight with adoration. "Best day ever. How are we going to top this?"

"Become circus performers?" Sydney suggested.

"I think joy has made you delirious."

"Every day since I was twelve. I can't believe we're finally officially married. We're going to have our own place and be alone. Isn't that a nice word? Alone."

"Don't say it again until we get to the hotel. I can't take it," Joe said. He glanced to the edge of the dance floor. "Hey, look, there's your good buddy, Cassius, waiting and hoping I step away to the bathroom for a second so he can hop in line and take my place. Keep waiting, buddy. I'll buy adult diapers, if I have to."

"Our wedding is a weird time for you to develop sudden jealousy," Sydney said.

"You think this is sudden? Oh, baby, no. I've been jealous of you every minute of every day since day one of seventh grade."

"Why have I never known this before?" she asked.

"Because I was trying to be suave and woo you," he said.

"And now the wooing is over?"

"Now the wooing moves to phase two."

"What's phase two?"

He leaned in her ear and whispered. She clutched his lapels. "Okay, back to phase one, at least until we reach the hotel. Have mercy, I still have to look your parents in the eye after this dance." She used his shirt to dab a bit of sweat on her forehead. Chuckling, he drew her impossibly closer.

"Let's make a baby plan," she said.

"What's a baby plan?"

"It's our plan to have a baby," she said.

"Okay, let's have a baby."

She rolled her eyes. "I have two years of college left, and then everyone tells me the first couple years of teaching are a nightmare."

"Sweetheart, it sounds like you already have a baby plan. Why don't you fill me in on what it is?"

"How about when we're twenty four? That gives us four years to enjoy some newlywed bliss."

"Perfection," he said.

"You like the plan?"

"No, I think you're perfection, the plan is up to you. I'll have a baby whenever you want, this minute, four years from now, ten. Don't care."

"Of course you care."

He shook his head. "Nothing is going to change for me. I'll work the same job that won't change, won't have to be pregnant. Nothing will change."

"Our marriage might change," she said, frowning.

He smoothed out her brow. "Our marriage won't change, we won't let it. Come on, Peaches, it's us. Everyone wants to be us. We're Joe and Peaches. This thing will never, ever, ever fall apart."

She grinned goofily up at him. "Yeah, I know. You should dance with your mom now, and I'll dance with your dad."

"Nope."

"But, Joe, it's proper."

"Don't care, not letting go, forever and ever."

"Amen," she said, standing on her toes to press impossibly closer.

CHAPTER 26

*S*ydney drove and drove. Her phone beeped with a text from an unknown number.

Hey, it's Cassius. I got your number from Sherry's phone, like the creepy guy I am now. But I have a legit reason for texting. Forgot to ask if there is anything you can do to get my middle kid in your class next year? It's her dream among dreams to be in your class, and I would be a total hero if I had a hand in getting her in with THE Mrs. Samperi.

Impossibly, Sydney smiled. *I'll have a word with my principal and see what I can do. But you're a cop. Doesn't that already guarantee hero status?*

You'd think so, but no. Still waiting on that coffee....

Her thumb hovered over the phone. She was tempted, more tempted than she'd ever been before. It would be so easy to suggest a meeting, to take comfort in Cassius who, she knew, would provide it so willingly. With a shake of her head, she tossed the phone aside and pressed the gas pedal, gunning it to she knew not where.

When she finally arrived at the destination she hadn't known she was heading toward, she chuckled. Of course. Where else?

She peeled herself out of the car, walked up the to the porch, and knocked. Marie opened the door, looking as stern and upset as Sydney had ever seen her.

"I heard," were her first words. They looked at each other a few beats, and then Sydney burst into tears and propelled herself forward, into Marie's waiting arms.

"Mama."

Marie led her to the couch and held her for a long, long time while she wept and wept. It seemed she cried not just for what happened tonight, but for everything that had ever happened to her in her life. Marie held her and let it happen, smoothing the wet hair off her face, running her hand up and down her back, murmuring motherly words of comfort. When it seemed she was all cried out, she put her arm around her shoulders and gave them a squeeze.

"Come on, your old room is all ready for you."

Sydney sat up. "You're not going to make me go home to him?"

"Not before I have a go at him with my spoon."

Sydney sputtered a laugh.

Marie gave her another squeeze. "I need to say something, something I maybe should have said a long time ago but, believe it or not, I didn't want to interfere." She took a bracing breath. "Things between you and Joe haven't been right for a long time, I know, Pete knows, we all know. I hope and pray things will work out between you, but if not I need you to know you will always, always be ours. From the moment Joe brought you home in seventh grade and introduced his Peaches, you became our girl. You may not be the child of my body, but you are the child of my heart. That will never change, no matter what."

Impossibly, Sydney found more tears. She hugged Marie and cried some more. It was the biggest relief of her life to understand that, regardless of how things turned out with Joe, she would always be a Samperi, no matter what. "This family is the best thing that ever happened to me, and you're the mom of my heart, forever."

Marie kissed both cheeks and her forehead. They turned toward the stairs when the front door banged open and Joe entered, his voice wild with panic and calling her name.

"Sydney, Sydney. Is she here? Sydney." He spilled into the room, his eyes as wild as his words. "You have to come home."

"No, she doesn't," Marie said, arm tightening on Sydney's shoulders.

"Out of it, Ma."

"No. You can't kiss another woman then show up here and drag her away, I won't allow it. You go away and think about your shameful, cowardly behavior, Joseph Samperi. I'll deal with you later." She turned Sydney toward the stairs, but Sydney remained frozen.

She closed her eyes, took a deep breath, opened her eyes, and faced her husband. "I should go with Joe. We have some things to discuss."

He had been crying, was still crying, great tears trailing down his cheeks and plopping on his chest. Even his tears were oversized. Sydney's heart tugged at the sight, mad and hurt as she was.

"Are you sure, Peaches? You can stay, you're always welcome here," Marie said.

Sydney squeezed her hand. "I appreciate that, Marie, but my place is with Joe, at least for the time being until we get some things figured out."

Marie gave a little nod and took a step back.

"I'll meet you at home," Sydney said.

"I...I don't think I can drive. I don't actually know how I got here," Joe said. He pressed his keys into her hand.

She stared at the keys and then at him. She never drove, ever. Since they were sixteen, he was always the driver, if they were together. "All right." She took another breath and led the way to the car.

"Peaches," he tried when they were in the car.

She shook her head.

He faced forward, taking quavering little breaths that occasionally ended on a sob. "How am I suddenly the strong one in this relationship?" She had no idea she said it out loud, meant to say it only in her head, until Joe answered.

"You've always been the strong one."

She shook her head like a dog ridding itself of water. They arrived home and trooped inside, Joe following at her heels like a puppy. He paused in the living room. She took his hand and led him to the bedroom.

He stood in the center of their room, eyes squinting in confusion as she reached for his shirt and began to undress him.

"What are you doing?" he asked.

"What I should have done a long time ago. I'm erasing this stupid space between us, and then afterwards we'll talk." She finished removing his shirt and reached for her own, lifting it over her head while he watched her with wide eyes. When they were fully undressed she kissed him, not because she particularly wanted to, but because she needed to. It had been the worst day of her life, and she needed her person, even if he was the person who caused the hurt. She was tired, so tired of running away from him instead of toward him. It was his fault he kissed some girl, but it was her fault for pushing him toward her, for pushing him away. And so she was claiming responsibility for her part of things the only way she knew how at the moment.

Joe responded, as she knew he would, as he always did, no matter how upset or angry or hurt. He couldn't resist her, and there was some power in that. A lot of power, if she were being honest.

"Did you lose weight?" he murmured, his lips moving against hers.

"Twelve pounds," she replied.

"Why? You're perfect, so perfectly perfect."

Those were the last words either of them spoke for a while.

Later, they curled on their sides, facing each other, not saying a word, staring with wide eyes and serious faces. Even so, some cracks had been sealed between them. Finally Joe swallowed hard and reached out, clasping her hand. "I love you so much, Syd. So, so much. I always have, I always will."

"I love you, too, Joe, you know that."

"Why does it feel like there's a 'but' in there?"

"Because there is. I love you, but I don't know if love is enough anymore."

Tears filled his eyes, and her eyes, too. "Because of what I did? Because of tonight?"

She shook her head.

"Because we can't have babies?"

"Because of everything, but mostly because of me."

"Don't you want me anymore?" he asked.

"Yes, I do. But…" she took a breath and made herself say it. "Ever since we met, I've had this fear that you were going to reach a limit with me, that you were going to get tired of my insecurity, my sadness, and go away. It seemed like having babies was the one thing I could give you in return for all the hard work you were doing on my behalf. And then when I couldn't… I've felt so guilty and ashamed, Joe. I've felt like such a failure, you have no idea. The weight of it, it's crushing. And then I started having this awful anxiety that you would meet someone else, someone younger and fertile who could give you babies. You would go off and start your life with her, and I would be this tragic footnote, your first love, your high school sweetheart."

It felt good to say it, to unburden herself from the awful truth, all the horrible, negative self-talk and doubts she'd harbored these many years. Joe didn't reply for a solid minute, merely stared at her, mouth agape and speechless.

"I don't…I don't know what to say. All this time I thought you resented me."

She blinked. "Resented you? Why would I resent you?"

"Because I couldn't give you the kind of life you wanted, a grand adventure. Because we were stuck here in our town with my family constantly trying to intrude. Because I couldn't give you the kind of family you longed for."

Now it was her turn to be speechless for a bit. "Joe, I've never felt any of those things, not for a minute, not for one iota."

"And I've never felt any of those things about you. Peaches, if for some nightmare reason this doesn't work out, I will never marry again. I could never, would never. It would be a betrayal to you, to us, to everything I've ever held dear. And, while we're on the subject, we can't fall apart, we just can't. I won't allow it, I wouldn't survive it. For two thirds of my entire life, there has only ever been you beside me. I don't know how to exist without you, and I don't want to try."

"I hate what we've become," she whispered.

"So do I, but I love you, I love you so much, even more than before.

You've grown even better with age. And, girl, you're hot." He reached out and gathered her close, lavishing her face with teary kisses.

She laughed, but she was crying, too. "I'm sorry. I'm sorry I've held myself away from you and been stuck in this rut of depression. I'm sorry I pushed you away and lashed out and cocooned myself in my grief alone." Her hand caressed his face.

"I'm sorry. I'm sorry I let you go, didn't keep up pursuing you, resented you for feeling sad. And..." he paused and sucked a deep breath. "I'm sorry I kissed another woman. I can't even believe I'm saying those words." He swiped a hand over his face. "I'm sick, so sick at myself. I can't believe it happened. I don't understand what happened."

"While we're confessing, I should probably tell you I've been talking some with Cassius. Nothing has happened, but it feels like I'm teetering on the edge, like if I gave him any sort of signal, it would be on."

He threw off the covers, darted from the bed, and skittered into the bathroom. Sydney heard him heave into the commode before it flushed. He brushed his teeth and returned to bed, settling down beside her without a word.

"We should probably talk some more," he said after a time.

"Probably, but for now would you just hold me? I miss you so much." She started to cry again, gently this time, and he did, too. He reached for her and drew her close, tucking her against him the way he used to, so he fully surrounded her, so she was comfortable in his embrace. She trembled, her heart racing with the memory of his nearness. His hand was twined together between both of hers. He used his free hand to push her hair aside and sang her a little song, directly in her ear, just for her. "You are my sunshine..."

In the morning, things were different. Awkwardness and space tried to intrude between them. Joe could sense Sydney struggling to pull away. He captured her hand and held it against his chest.

"I'm sorry, Syd. I'm so sorry. If I could take it back, I would."

"Is she pretty?" she asked.

He nodded. "But not as pretty as you, and I'm not just saying that. You are the most beautiful girl in the world to me, always."

"But you are attracted to her," she said.

"I mean, I guess. Not in any lasting way. You see someone, you get a flicker, you move on." He paused. "Are you attracted to Cassius?"

"In the same way, I suppose. He's a handsome man."

"If you like that sort," he said sourly.

"More, I liked that he listened, and I like the way he sees me."

"How's that?" he asked.

"Strong, capable, good."

He propped himself on an elbow. "I see you as all of those things, and a whole bunch more."

"But how could you? You know me better than anyone, know I'm not actually any of those things. I'm, well, I'm a mess."

"Everyone's a mess if you peel back enough layers," he said.

She was about to protest, to say he wasn't a mess, but he had kissed another woman. She frowned at the ceiling, thinking. What if everything she'd believed her whole life wasn't actually true? And, if it wasn't, what was true? If not Joe, if not their marriage, what could she rely on?

"Peaches, please don't give up on me, on us," he pled.

"I don't want to, but…"

"But what?"

"I'm so tired of everything being an uphill struggle, Joe. You were the one thing in life that wasn't supposed to be, the one thing that was supposed to be a given. And now somehow our marriage has become the hardest part. How can that be?"

"I don't know," he said quietly. "All I know is what we have is worth fighting for, worth protecting. If we're working together, if we're on each other's sides and have each other's backs, we're unstoppable. We've proved that. We can go back to how it was before."

Sydney didn't reply, but she wasn't certain they could ever go back.

And she wasn't certain she wanted to go forward, only to have it feel like it had felt the last few years. And yet she couldn't imagine life without him. There seemed to be no clear or good answer.

"I should go. I don't want to face up to what needs to happen today."

"What are you going to do?" she asked.

"Fire her, obviously, with a generous severance. I mean, what else is there? More than that, though, I hate the thought of facing my brothers and sister."

Sydney understood. To them, Joe had always been perfect. To her, too. Maybe it had been unfair of all of them to demand that sort of perfection from him. "I bet you'll be surprised by how much grace they give. You've always been their combined favorite."

"You, too," he said, pulling her on top of him, tucking his leg around her. "They're kind of like our first kids, in a way." His busy parents had left them often in their care.

"I used to pretend, before we started dating, before we confessed our feelings for each other, back when we used to insist we were only friends. I used to pretend we were married and they were our kids."

"I did, too," he said.

She smiled, remembering how it was to be young and giddily in love. Joe had been through every iteration of her life after early childhood. If she closed her eyes, she could remember exactly how he looked at that age, brown hair flopping over his eyes, on purpose so he could hide. All the girls had been crazy for him, and he had somehow picked her, Sydney Parker. Not just picked her, but gave her an epic nickname and attached himself to her with a vengeance. She was the only person outside his family who knew what the barn looked like before it was renovated, who remembered when the family used to sleep in tents while Pete worked on the renovation, who knew how tight their finances were before the business took off. Money had never been an issue between them because, for that first little bit in the beginning, they were both the same: poor.

"What'd you find to smile about?"

"Twelve year old you."

"Twelve year old you always makes me smile, too. But then you at any age makes me smile, Peaches." He blew out a breath. "I screwed everything up, everything with you, everything with my family, everything with my job."

"I'm still here, Joe. Your family will still be here. Your job will still be here." She paused. "Do you want me to go with you to the office, present a united front?"

"You would do that?" he asked, awed.

"Yes."

He swiped his hand over his eyes. "No. I mean, yes, I would love to have you with me, but no, it's my mess and unfair to make you step in it. I'll handle it."

"It's going to be okay," she said because, even in the midst of her own hurt, she wanted him to feel better, needed to reassure him life would be okay again and he would bounce back. "I'm not trying to make this all about me, but I do want you to understand. This feeling you're feeling right now, of grief and shame and embarrassment, that's what I've been feeling every day of the last twelve years."

He sucked a breath. "Peaches, that's awful. But why? Why would you feel that way, baby girl? It's not your fault we can't have kids."

"Because I'm the woman. It's my body that's malfunctioning, even if we don't have a name for why. I'm failing at the most basic part of being a girl."

"I have never once thought that of you, ever. It's different for us, I see that now, but please believe me that I in no way blame you for our inability to have a child, not even a little."

"I wanted us to be a family." She sniffled.

"Peaches, we *are* a family. You and me, we've always been our own bubble, our own circle, our own tribe." He gripped her shoulders tight, giving her a little shake. "*We are a family,* a family of two. Don't discount what's between us because it's a smaller number than you want it to be."

She nodded and pressed her face to his neck, letting his reassurance wash over her and scrub away the years of pain and insecurity.

CHAPTER 27

Sydney arrived on Chrissy's doorstep, bag in hand. She wore the expression of someone who needed a long and heartfelt talk, so Chrissy turned and led the way to her kitchen table.

"What's up?" she asked as she pulled out a chair and sat down.

"Joe kissed his secretary."

Chrissy dashed to her feet so quickly her chair toppled backwards. She reached for a wicked looking boning knife. "Where's he working today? I'll make it look like an accident."

"We're working through it," Sydney said.

Chrissy regarded her a minute, frowning, assessing how sincerely she meant it. She lay the knife on the table and sat down. "What happens now?"

"I thought we'd eat ice cream, straight from the carton." She set the bag she'd brought between them and removed two pints of ice cream.

"This is why we're friends," Chrissy said. She reached into a drawer and pulled out two spoons, plastic because she hated doing dishes so much she had no permanent silverware.

"You know what I want? I want to go one day without feeling like I'm getting broadsided in the face with a shovel by one of life's little catastrophes," Sydney said, loading her spoon with a mass dose of peanut butter fudge ripple.

"At least you still have all your teeth. You've been able to maintain that pretty homecoming queen smile," Chrissy said.

Sydney stuck her hand in the air, smiled, and gave a beauty queen wave.

"That's right, princess. Smile at infertility," Chrissy commanded.

Sydney tipped her head and smiled wider, waving with more intensity.

"Now smile at the media that's going to start poking into your personal life once they get wind of it, which they most assuredly will," Chrissy said.

Sydney smiled so hard it hurt, waving frantically now.

"Smile at all those women from all those charity functions who are going to glory in your demise."

Sydney smiled and waved, then thought better of it and flicked her fingers under her chin in a gesture Joe taught her in seventh grade.

"That's better," Chrissy said, nodding her approval. "Now smile at your husband's mistress."

Sydney snatched the knife and made a jabbing motion in the air.

"There's my girl," Chrissy said happily.

They ate in silence a while until Sydney's phone buzzed. She picked it up and read with a sigh.

"What now?" Chrissy asked.

"It's Cassius." She read his text out loud. "Syd, just heard something about you and Joe. Call me ASAP. Worried about you." She set the phone down. "You were right about him, he's interested. And you were right about me. I'm vulnerable, and he's attractive and attentive." She handed Chrissy her phone. "Do what you will, Accountability Guru."

Gleefully, Chrissy took the phone and fired off a text. Wincing preemptively, Sydney picked it up and read it.

Thanks for your concern, but I'm working on my marriage with my husband and cannot contact you anymore. Please respect my wishes and don't text again.

"Huh," Sydney said. "I kind of thought you'd go nuclear on him."

"He seems like a nice guy. Not his fault he got Sydney'd. Although I did block him, so if he makes contact some other way let me know and, well, you know." She picked up the knife again and gave a few jabs.

They finished their ice cream and Sydney pressed her hands to her stomach, half-sick but also better somehow.

"What now?" Chrissy asked.

"I have some shower stuff to go over with you." She reached for a second bag containing her notebook and laptop.

"That's still on?" Chrissy asked.

"Samperi for life, baby," Sydney said.

"You know I'm all in, but you also know the entire day is going to be people looking at you, pitying you, studying your face and reactions to everything."

"Bring it," Sydney said. "Peaches 2.0. doesn't care what people think about her."

"Finally, a Peaches I can get on board with," Chrissy said. She reached for Sydney's ice ream container and scraped all the bits she'd missed. "What's next? With you and Joe, I mean."

"I don't know. I really don't know," Sydney said, but she felt strangely calm and at peace, probably because, no matter what, Chrissy was always on her side. Having someone to count on made all the difference. Joe used to be that person for her, and she for him. How must he be feeling right now, at work and facing everything alone without her? She shouldn't have let him go on his own. Frantically, she stood and began throwing things into her bag.

"Mental breakdown?" Chrissy guessed.

"No, I've had enough of those for a lifetime. This is me, finally getting it together."

"Hallelujah, girl. Call if you need backup," Chrissy said.

"You can't go where I'm about to tread. Love ya," Sydney said. She leaned down, kissed the top of her friend's head, and jetted from the house.

*P*eaches let herself into Joe's office and saw him staring at his desk. He glanced up at her with a smile, eyes snapping into focus.

"Hey," she said.

His smile widened. "Do you purposely do that to me?"

"What?" she asked, confused.

"Say 'hey' exactly as you did on that first day, all those years ago, so I lose my heart again every single time."

"No, but that's handy information to have in my arsenal."

"Your arsenal couldn't possibly get any bigger. At this point you're stockpiling. Whatcha got going on today?"

"I ate an entire pint of ice cream," she said.

"It looks good on you."

"Thank you. But now I'm feeling the need to burn it off, but I can't go to my gym anymore."

"Why not?"

"It's Cassius's gym."

"Let's burn it down," Joe suggested. "Also, we have that home gym in the basement."

"Yes, but I like to exercise with others." She reached behind herself, unzipped her dress, and stepped out of it.

Joe swallowed hard, transfixed. "What's going on? Because this is the second day in a row you've taken off your clothes with no coaxing from me, and I want you to know I am here for it."

She walked behind his desk, pushed him away from it, and sat in his lap. "Remember when we were first married and I used to show up at your worksites wearing a dress with nothing underneath?"

"It's permanently branded into my brain." His hands were already busy caressing her.

"And then sometimes when you had to be in the office working late, I'd bring you supper and we'd put some more scratches and scars in this oak." She tapped the desk.

"This is the best walk down memory lane I've ever been on," he informed her.

"Why did we stop doing that?"

"I have no idea," he said.

"All my friends who have kids always tell me how exhausted they are, how hard it is to find time to be a couple when they're busy trying to be parents. But you and I have no children. The one upside to infertility is all our vast energy and time. We should be mating like bunnies."

Joe nodded his enthusiastic agreement. She reached for the remote to the radio she'd bought him for this very purpose. It had been far too long since they used it. "Jazz?" she grimaced. "Why jazz? You hate that."

"Because it's loud and, sweetheart, so are you." He lifted her onto his oversized desk and set her down, leaning over her. "I think if we've learned one thing from dancing, it's that things go better when I lead."

"Big talk for a man still wearing all his clothes." She tugged his shirt.

"Right, right." Frantic now, he stood upright and tugged his shirt, which got immediately stuck on his head. "I'm going to rip it off."

She sat up. "No, don't. Your mom will see it when she does the laundry and she'll know."

"How would she know?"

"She's knows things. She knows everything," Sydney whispered.

"Then help me."

She reached out a hand and brushed his stomach, causing him to suck in a sharp breath. "I don't know. I kind of like you at my mercy this way."

"Peaches," he implored, sounding pained.

"All right," she agreed and began unbuttoning his shirt. She finished and tossed the shirt aside. He put his arms around her and pressed her back into the desk.

"Hey."

"Hey."

"In case I didn't tell you today, I love you."

"Let's employ a show-don't-tell policy for the remainder of this day," she said.

"Yes, ma'am," he agreed and kissed her.

A long time later they emerged from his office, pausing in the doorway to giggle and smooch like the teenagers they once were. Someone cleared his throat and they jumped to attention.

All of Joe's siblings stood in a line, facing them, arms crossed, looking severe.

"What have you guys been doing?" Moss asked. Joe straightened and began tucking in his shirt, but Peaches put her hands on her hips. The effect was ruined when Joe reached over and zipped the last four inches of her dress.

"It makes me feel like Maria von Trapp when y'all stand in a line that way, like you're waiting for inspection. Nails out, let's see them. And of course you know what we've been doing. Y'all are having babies."

Grinning, they dutifully stuck their nails out for her inspection. She went first to Benny, grasping his hand and turning it over. "These hands are looking soft. Time to pick up a hammer, little brother." She stood on her toes and kissed his cheek. To Jessamine, she exclaimed, "Oh, girl, I love this manicure." She kissed her cheek and moved on to Giovanni, inspecting his perfect fingers. "Giovanni, you look like you could be giving manicures." She kissed his cheek and moved on to Moss, gasping. "Child, wash your hands." Moss picked her up and spun her in circles.

"Peaches, Peaches, Peaches, Peaches." He set her down and kissed her cheek. She swiped beneath her teary eyes and took a steadying breath.

"I sure do love y'all," she said, smiling.

"We love you," Giovanni agreed.

"Best big sister ever," Benny added.

She blew them a kiss and let herself out of the office. They turned to Joe who attempted to straighten and right his shirt again, without success.

"Why are you still here? Go get your woman," Giovanni commanded.

"I still have work to..." Joe began, the grinned. "Nah, forget it. I'll see you. Someone turn off my radio." He tossed his keys in the air, caught them, and sprinted after his wife.

The mood after they departed was somber. It had been a hard morning for all of them. Joe was their idol, and it hurt to see him diminished.

"I haven't seen them like that in so long," Jessamine breathed. She started to cry, and Benny pulled her into a hug.

"Do you think they're fixed now?" Moss asked hopefully.

"I hope so, but I doubt it, at least not yet. If I did what Joe did, Vivian would eviscerate me," Giovanni said.

Moss pulled out a tissue and handed it to his sister. "Jess, please stop crying or Milo is going to burst in, gun drawn, and start demanding answers." She gave a watery little laugh and wiped her nose.

"I want them to be how they were," Giovanni said. "So in love it hurt to look at them, and all you wanted was to find what they had." His voice broke, and he crossed his arms, scowling.

Moss perched on the edge of the desk beside him, deflated. "I won't be a Samperi anymore if Peaches goes."

"You'll still be a Samperi, just a heartbroken one," Giovanni said sadly.

"I feel like we should do something to help them," Jessamine said.

"So do I," Benny agreed. Everyone faced him, the de facto leader when Joe was away.

"Do you have an idea?" Jessamine asked.

"Maybe. I'll have to check into some things, but it would require a massive sacrifice on all our parts," he said.

Moss stood and stuck out his hand. "For Joe and Peaches."

"For Joe and Peaches," Giovanni agreed, laying his on top.

"Joe and Peaches," Jessamine and Benny agreed, adding their hands to the pile.

CHAPTER 28

Sydney and Joe sat cuddled on the couch, watching mindless television. Neither could remember the last time they did something so mundane. Both of them were exhausted by recent events. Absently, Joe reached for one of her notebooks from the table beside them and picked it up.

"What's this?"

Sydney glanced at it. "My bucket list for the infertile, stuff Chrissy and I are going to do together to pull me out of my funk and re-establish my identity as a functioning human." Her attention returned to the TV, but Joe continued to read.

"Parachute, bungee jump, zipline, shopping in Manhattan, weekend in Paris."

"Some of them might be a bit farfetched. Can't exactly imagine Chrissy in Paris, unless it's to nosh on cheese all weekend," Sydney murmured. When Joe didn't reply, she turned to look at him and saw him staring at the list, gripping it tightly. "What?"

He swallowed hard and set it aside. "This was all the stuff we used to talk about doing together."

"Does that hurt your feelings?"

"No. Yes, a little. But it's more than that. It makes me feel so guilty, like such a failure as a husband. I used to be your person, Peaches. The person you turned to when you were upset and the person you turned to when you wanted to have fun. And now that's Chrissy for you."

"Maybe it was unrealistic for us to believe we could continue to be everything to each other, for the remainder of our lives," Sydney suggested gently. "It's a lot to put on a person, Joe. Best friend, husband, counselor. I should never have counted on you to be my security, to try and cure me, to make me strong and emotionally healthy."

"Shouldn't you? If not, what's the point? And I indisputably let you down."

"No, you didn't," she argued. "My issues were deep, deep wounds that went far beyond the scope of infertility."

He shook his head. "I did, Syd, I know I let you down because I could feel myself doing it, but we were so happy, so solid, so settled. I let myself believe helping my dad with the business was more important, was higher priority. I took us for granted, and it's my fault we're in this situation now because I let things slip, didn't keep working on them."

"I would venture to say we both share the blame, Joe. I wanted you to fix me, counted on you to make things better, put too much hope in your ability to do so. And then when it didn't work, I resented you for it, pushed you away."

"I let you. I threw myself into work to avoid you. It was a handy excuse to always be so busy because I was being a good son. But in the meantime I was being a terrible husband."

"You haven't been a terrible husband," she said.

He reached for her list and held it aloft again. "We haven't done any of these things. I haven't kept any of the promises I made to you. Magic, what a joke." He pressed his hand to his eyes.

"Most people don't have magic all the time," she said in the same soft tone.

"But we were supposed to be better than everybody else. We were supposed to have a grand and epic love affair, and look at us."

"Let's look at us," Sydney said. She took his hand and gave it a squeeze. "Still together after twenty four years, married sixteen. Still in love, still friends, still crazy attracted to each other. Is it a laugh a minute? A barrel of fun? No. But do we keep getting back up after life keeps knocking us down? I hope so. I'm trying to. I want you beside me when I do."

"I want to be the one pulling you up, not the one knocking you down, making you hurt. I want to be your champion and protector."

"You always have been. Maybe it needs a little tweaking, but we'll keep working on it." She rested her head on his shoulder.

He kissed the top of her head. "I love you, Peaches. But I've been thinking about what you said, and it takes more than loving. I thought that was enough, got lazy in our relationship, but no more. I don't know what the answer is, but I'm looking for it. And I'm going to keep trying. From now on you are my first priority, not my family, not my job. Only you. I'm sorry you weren't those things before when you should have been."

"I'm sorry I made you think you had to be perfect for me, to be my savior. I'm not going to do that anymore, not going to put all that on you. We'll be friends and lovers and husband and wife, not psychiatrist and patient, not hero and damsel."

"I like fixing you, saving you. It only goes sideways when I feel like I can't."

"Maybe I'll let you save me sometimes, to keep you feeling special. But I'm getting better at saving myself. The thing I'm learning is that when life gives you the worst thing you can possibly imagine and it doesn't break you, you come out stronger on the other side."

"Rise, queen," he said, and she giggled.

"Please never say that again."

"Deal." He settled her more comfortably in his embrace and they continued to do nothing at all. It was, hands down for both of them, the best night in recent memory.

A few days later Sydney woke in the night and crept to the bathroom, being careful not to disturb Joe. By now she had it down to a routine, could do it so soundlessly and sneakily he had no idea.

She reached to the back of the vanity, to her private and secret stash, and pulled out a test. She tore open the package, feeling a secret little thrill, and held the test aloft. And then she stared at it, frozen.

Her period was four days late, her breasts tender and swollen. She could be pregnant this time, she really could. All she had to do was take the test, pee on the stick, and within two minutes she'd know.

Instead she tucked it back into the package, returned to her room, sat on the bed, and shook Joe's shoulder. "Joey."

"Hmm," he grunted, still asleep.

"I have a problem."

He rallied slightly, peering at her through a squinty glance. "Hmm."

"I'm addicted to peeing on strips of paper."

He sat up and swiped a hand over his face. "Honey, what?"

She swallowed hard and dumped the bag between them.

"What's all this?" he asked.

"A hundred unopened pregnancy tests."

"Why so many?" he asked.

"Because I never believe them. Any time I'm a few days late, I take one, and when it's negative I'm certain it's wrong. So I take another, and then another, and then as many as it takes until I get my period. And then I cry and grieve and mourn."

"How often does this happen?" he asked.

"Every month for the last twelve years," she said.

He swallowed hard and dashed at his eyes. "How can I help?"

She pulled her knees up to her chest and wrapped her arms around them. "I'm so tired of being on this rollercoaster, Joe. So tired of waiting and hoping and being crushed when it doesn't happen. I want to get off the ride."

He reached for her and bundled her close, still curled up like a pill bug. His arms were long enough to contain all of her, and he held her tightly, raining kisses on her face. "Okay."

She took a shaky breath. "It's not as simple as throwing this away. It means coming to terms with the reality that I will never have a baby, your baby. We will never be parents to our biological child. Don't take it lightly, please. Don't say a flippant okay because you want to fix me."

He took a deep, shaky breath and let it out slowly. "Peaches, it's different for us. I don't have the biological pull toward children you do. Would I love them? Yes. Have I been in mourning because we can't? Maybe a little. But I do have a biological pull toward you, toward your heart and happiness. That is my mission and only goal in life, to ease your broken pieces and try to fit them back together. I haven't always done the best job of that, but that changes today. So let's get off the roller coaster together, and from this moment on, I swear to you our marriage will be what it should have been all along. Our lives will be what we want them to be. Because I would rather have you than ten thousand children. You are my heart, my world, and I love you more than anything on this earth." He kissed her, exactly as he used to when they were kids, and she believed him. She wept, but it was with a sense of relief and release. She was done grieving and ready to live her life with Joe, however that looked in the future.

He took the tests to the outside trashcan, and when he returned, he had her suitcase in hand. "Get packed, we're going on an adventure."

Sydney sat up, feeling impossibly light hearted. They were immersed in the biggest crisis of their marriage, and she was still infertile. But something had changed between them, something had been renewed. For the first time in a long, long time, she felt hopeful about their future, optimistic about the long road ahead. Giggling, she bounded out of bed and began tossing items in her suitcase, her heart happier than it had been for as long as she could remember.

CHAPTER 29

For their honeymoon, Joe and Peaches spent ten days in Italy, a leisurely trip to see the countryside and visit Joe's family.

The weekend he took her on an adventure, their first in years, they flew to Florence for a whirlwind tour. They ate, slept, talked, explored, ate, slept, and talked some more. They didn't visit Joe's Zia. They didn't do anything that wasn't for them. It was restorative, fun, and exhausting, albeit in a good way.

They arrived home ready to face everything that awaited, not realizing a new situation had developed while they were away.

Chrissy was the one to break the first bit of bad news. Sydney received a text from her as soon as they entered the states and she turned her phone back on.

Practice your smile and wave. The media knows.

Sydney sighed. It was probably too much to hope it would remain secret. Ever since the television show started, people had been fascinated with their family. When the initial burst of fame happened, they had nosed around, looking for stories or scandals. There had been some fascination with her and Joe's love story—*Middle School Sweethearts! Two Decades Together And Still In Love!* But as neither she nor Joe ever gave an interview, things soon died down. And then Jessamine acquired a stalker and married her bodyguard, and the frenzy started all over again. It had finally started to die, and now this. The calls would start again, people camped in front of their house. Joe's phone beeped with a call from the home and garden channel, wanting a comment.

"It will blow over," Sydney assured him with more confidence than she felt. And it also poked at a tender spot. There was a part of her that still couldn't believe Joe had done it, that hadn't yet begun to get over the hurt of his betrayal. Joe stared straight ahead, jaw set, and she knew what he was thinking. He was harder on himself than anyone, was livid with himself over his mistake. And now the world would know, and his family would be in the spotlight. It was almost more than he could bear.

Sydney burrowed under his arm, pressing close until he unbent and hugged her in return. "It's going to be fine," she assured him.

"It's not fair to you."

"Hey, still beats infertility," she said and meant it. She had started her period in Italy. The pain of that pinched, but it was nowhere near the tidal wave of grief it usually was. Sydney had still been able to laugh, to think of other things, to practice letting it go.

The next bit of bad news came from Benny, a group text to everyone.

We're being sued. Samantha Rogers is suing the company for wrongful termination and Joe personally for sexual harassment.

"What?" Joe exclaimed, incensed as he stared at his phone. "Sexual harassment? I barely talked to her before that day, and certainly never touched her. That's crazy."

The news spread like wildfire, so quickly Chrissy was waiting on their doorstep when they arrived home.

"What do you need?" she asked Sydney.

"At this point, I don't even know," Sydney replied, snagging her arm and tugging her inside behind her. Joe bypassed them, locking himself in their room. "He feels bad. What a mess."

Chrissy opened the freezer, withdrew ice cream, grabbed two

spoons, and set it on the table between them. "Something is wrong with this whole situation."

"I'll say."

"No, I mean really. I don't like many men, but I do like Joe. He's one of the good ones, stupid mistake notwithstanding. No way he assaulted or harassed this girl. I mean, how long was she at the company? A minute?"

"This is why you're a good sounding board, because I was having these thoughts, but they felt biased by my deep dislike of her."

"You need to be proactive. Time to fight back."

"Please tell me this isn't going to end with you staked out under her bed with a knife," Sydney said.

"She would never see me coming,"

"Would it be too crazy scorned wife if I hired a private investigator to look into things?"

"What would Peaches 2.0 do?"

"Probably go to her house and have an old-fashioned come-to-Jesus talk with her myself."

"Then an investigator seems like a reasonable next step, the sooner the better."

"How do you think you hire one of those?"

Chrissy pulled out her phone and they spent some time selecting whoever had the best ad and website. Thirty minutes later, Sydney had paid a two thousand dollar advance for information on Samantha Rogers.

"I feel so tawdry."

"It's an ironic fact that people who are tawdry likely never say the word tawdry," Chrissy said.

Someone knocked on the door.

"Now what?" Sydney muttered.

"I'll get it. Let me play maid of the manor," Chrissy said. She stood and smoothed a hand over her crew cut, giving a practice curtsy that made Sydney laugh.

"The maid in flannel, that's you," she said. She rested her head in her hand and stared into space until Chrissy returned, Moss and Molly in tow. At the sight of Molly, she stood.

"Sweet girl, what are you doing out and about? You should be home." Molly was still struggling with extreme nausea, could barely manage to keep so much as a sip of water down. Her tiny frame had grown tinier, a little bump her only outward sign of pregnancy.

"I'm doing fine, Peaches, thank you. I need to show you something, and it's too important to do it any way other than in person."

Moss held a chair for her. She sank gratefully into it and reached for her laptop. "Where's Joe? He should be a part of this, too."

"I'm here," Joe said from the doorway. "Are you sure you should be here? You look all done in."

"I'm fine," Molly insisted. She opened her computer and waited for it to wake up. "So, sometimes at work I put Bella down for a nap in Joe's office. I installed a nanny cam so I can keep an eye on her and continue to work. It's the kind that kicks on and records, archiving everything for about a day. It automatically deletes, unless I save it. When I heard what happened with my replacement, I thought it would be best to keep the recording, just in case. I want you to know I didn't watch it then, it seemed like an invasion. But when I heard about the lawsuit, I thought it was a good idea to see exactly what happened." She turned her computer to face them.

"Peaches shouldn't see this," Joe said, sounding strained.

"Yes, Peaches should. I am not a victim, and I want to know," she said. Even so, her stomach twisted up in knots. She wanted to know how bad things were, but her stomach might actually revolt watching Joe with another woman.

The screen flicked to life and showed Samantha enter Joe's office. He was standing, as if about to leave. They spoke for a minute, smiling, laughing, then she tipped forward and kissed him. A second later, he spun away and ran out of the room.

"Hold up," Sydney said, squinting. "Can you go back a few seconds?"

Molly complied, backing the video up a bit. Sydney leaned in and studied Joe's hands to see what they did when the kiss occurred. They came up, surprised, the way someone might if he accidentally smacked into someone, palms up and out like a stop sign. She burst into tears and rested her forehead on the table.

"Please, can we not," Joe said. He hurried forward and closed the laptop. "Syd, I'm sorry you had to see that."

She gripped his hand and sat up. "Joe, I'm not crying because I'm upset with you. I'm crying because I'm upset with me."

"Why?" he breathed.

"Because I believed you kissed that girl, even for a minute."

Joe scanned the room, as if seeking answers to his wife's mental health. No one had any answers, furthering his confusion. "But, Syd, I did. You saw."

"No, I saw *her* kiss *you*, unasked, unprovoked. I saw you respond as if you'd smacked into a wall and then run away. What happened after?"

"I threw up in the bushes and drove home to tell you." He sank into the chair beside her. "What are you saying, exactly? I'm so confused."

"I'm saying you didn't kiss her of your own volition, you didn't kiss her back, you didn't even continue the kiss once you realized it was happening. And you certainly didn't harass her. Either she's delusional or a predator," Sydney said.

"That's what Moss and I thought, too," Molly said.

Sydney reached over the table and squeezed Molly's hand. "Molly, as usual you are worth your weight in gold. Even when you're on medical leave you're the best secretary we have. We certainly were blessed the day you became a Samperi."

Molly blushed, eyes teary. Moss bundled her up and gave her a squeeze, kissing her cheeks. Their toddler, Bella, trundled over to Sydney and asked to be picked up. Sydney tugged her close with a kiss. "And this angel. What a crew y'all are. I can't wait to meet the new addition." She was relieved to know how much she meant it. She would love their new baby, all the new babies.

Beside her, Joe shifted uncomfortably. "Uh, sweetheart, all of that is so, so true, but *Molly has a camera in my office.*" He gave her a significant look.

"I know, and it's a good thing she..." She got it, all of a sudden, what he was trying to tell her. She had recently starred in one of Molly's videos. They faced her, cheeks flaming, at a loss for words.

Molly laughed. "I do get an alert whenever there's movement in that room. But as soon as I realized what was about to happen, I turned it off and closed my computer. I'm no voyeur. Y'all are safe."

"You might be safe from Molly's camera, but Jesus and Santa still know what you did," Moss said. He touched his two fingers to his eyes and pointed them across the table.

"They know what you did, too," Sydney said, pointing to Molly's baby bump.

Their company stayed for a while, talking and laughing. Sydney was palpably relieved by the new revelation. She felt like somehow everything would be okay now, regardless of the frivolous lawsuit. Joe, meanwhile, remained quiet and withdrawn.

Later, when they crawled sleepily into bed, jetlagged and exhausted, Sydney poked him. "What's wrong? You don't seem as relieved as I thought you would."

"No, I am, I guess. But if I'm being honest, I'm still guilty. Syd, I thought about kissing that girl, maybe wanted it to happen. I was tempted. Just because I wasn't the aggressor doesn't mean I wasn't complicit."

"I know that, Joe, I do. But it's so much less than what I thought it was. I thought," she paused and swallowed hard, "I really thought you took that girl in your arms, looked tender in her eyes, and pressed your lips to hers, with full intent, knowing what you were doing. That's something that's only been reserved for me, all these years. I'm glad I still have that. And, to be honest, we're both guilty of temptation. Those thoughts and feelings you described? Those are the same ones I had about Cassius. If I hadn't received a jolt, if we hadn't had this crisis thrust upon us, it might have been me in this situation. Who knows how far it might have gone?" They were both sick and silent, imagining how much worse everything might have been.

"How can something so bad end up so good?" he asked, reaching for her hand.

"I don't know, but it gives me a whole different perspective on infertility. I don't want to get my hopes up, but maybe…maybe all this hurt and all this pain is going to lead to something good, too. Maybe it's getting me ready for something bigger than I might have imagined."

"Magic," he said, squeezing her hand.

"Magic," she repeated, squeezing his in return. "My fear now is that I won't know it if it comes along, that I'll be too scared or too ignorant to recognize the good thing in front of me."

"I wouldn't worry, Peaches." He rolled over and faced her. "We have a pretty good track record of recognizing the best thing that could ever happen to us right away."

"True story," she said, rolling to face him. She trailed her finger down his face. "Hey."

He shook his head, smiling. "Gets me every single time." He reached for her and, exhausted and jetlagged as they were, it was a long time before they went to sleep.

CHAPTER 30

For a few days, Joe and Sydney couldn't leave home. Reporters camped at the end of their driveway and attempted to hound them every time they stepped outside.

"They probably think this bothers us," Sydney noted as they lay tucked cozily in bed, cups of coffee on a tray beside them.

"Little do they realize they're affording us a second honeymoon," Joe agreed. "I can't even remember the last time I slept in, let alone had more than one day off in a row."

She snuggled closer and rested her head on his chest. "You never had a choice about what you were going to do."

"I never wanted one. I love what I do, love working with my family."

"Do you love it, or did you try never to peer too closely at it so you wouldn't be discontent and resentful? Because you're always dutiful, Joey. Always the dedicated big brother, son, husband, employee. Setting all that aside and realizing you will continue to work for your family happily forever, is there a secret small part of you that wanted to do something else?"

"Whew, going deep, Peaches. I suppose it would have been fun to pursue something else, to spend more time with my artistic, creative side. There's a certain joy in construction, but it's fairly prescribed, not a lot of room for imaginative interpretation. I loved doing photography, but I always wanted to paint. And maybe play guitar. But working fulltime since I was fourteen hasn't left a lot of time for hobbies. Not that I'm complaining," he hastened to add.

"I know you're not. You're such a hard worker, Joe, such a good and consummate provider. Even in the beginning when we were starting out and didn't have much, I never faced the same sort of insecurity I felt growing up. I always knew you would take care of me. And I hope someday you get the chance to retire, to do things you want to do. Also, seeing you with that camera around your neck, always taking pictures. Whoo, so hot you made the backs of my knees sweat."

"Be right back, going to get my camera." He pretended to get up, and she tugged him back.

"As long as we're on the topic of careers, I'm not sure how much longer I'm going to stay in teaching."

"Really? It was always your dream."

"It was. I so badly wanted to make a difference, to make a lasting impact. But I don't think I am. My hands are tied by bureaucracy, and then I have to give those babies back to their terrible, sad situations. Time after time after time, year after year after year, and it hurts. Too much. I'd love to find somewhere more hands on, where I can make a bigger impact. But I don't know what that looks like yet."

"Maybe just quit, take some time off until you find something else."

"I'm just now getting back on my feet, getting in my groove. I'm afraid of too much free time, afraid I'll languish and fall back into destructive habits."

"Speaking of languishing, how much longer can we lie here before Milo and Jess show up for brunch?"

The doorbell rang. "About now. Could you grab that while I get presentable?" Not waiting for an answer, she kissed him and sprinted toward the bathroom.

A short time later, she emerged and gave hugs all around—to Jessamine, Milo, and Milo's teenaged daughter, Iz. Lunch had been

Jessamine's suggestion. For whatever reason she had seemed clingier lately, weepier, too. Sydney wasn't certain if it was because she was upset about all the recent events or feeling emotional over her pending delivery. Whatever the reason, she became teary whenever she happened to glance at Sydney or Joe, prompting her husband to reach out and rub a soothing little circle on her back. It was so far outside of her normal behavior that Sydney and Joe exchanged questioning glances. *Do you know what's up with her? No idea.*

They were almost finished with lunch when Chrissy texted.

Turn on the TV.

If it had been anyone else, Sydney wouldn't have listened. But Chrissy was neither hyperbolic nor dramatic. If she said the TV needed to be watched, the TV needed to be watched. Sydney reached for the remote and turned on the television. Joe's face stared back at her, a picture from a few years ago, a rough looking candid that seemed to have captured him mid-yawn so it looked like he was angry and yelling. A woman's voice spoke. Joe tensed, and the picture switched to her, Samantha Rogers. She sounded tearful, but it was amazing how none of those tears marred her perfect makeup. Sydney picked up the remote again and adjusted the volume so they could hear better.

"...Went to work for the Samperis because I loved the family so much, enjoyed watching them on TV. Let me tell you they are nothing like they appear. Rude, standoffish, volatile, angry. I began to fear for my safety. And then...and then that day. You have to understand Joe is a large and powerful man. I was so frightened." She paused to press the handkerchief to her face, shoulders shaking.

Chrissy texted again.

Psycho hose beast.

Everyone turned to look at Peaches like she'd flipped her lid when she chortled. "Chrissy," she explained, holding the phone aloft. Her laughter died when Jessamine started to cry.

"This is all my fault," she said. "If I hadn't gotten us on the stupid show and gotten all this publicity, this never would have happened."

Sydney's phone buzzed with a text from Molly.

This is all my fault. I shouldn't have taken sick leave.

"No, let's all be honest," Joe said. "This is all my fault, and now I've dragged everyone down with me."

Sydney slammed the phone onto the table, pushed away, and stood. "That about does it. Jess, straighten your crown, Princess. This is not on you. Can I borrow your lipstick, please? I'm in the mood for red." She held out her hand. Jessamine withdrew her ruby red lipstick and handed it over. Sydney stooped to look in the microwave as she applied it. Iz watched her with big eyes. She turned and swiped a little on the girl's lips, tossing her a wink before she handed it back.

"Iz, sweetheart, can you do me a favor?"

"Yes, ma'am," Iz said, squirming with excitement to be involved in whatever was now about to happen.

"See that blue flowered tray over there against the wall? Please set it out and fill it with as many cans of Coke as you can find in the fridge."

"Okay," Iz said, hopping up to do her bidding.

"Joe, please get me a piece of paper and a pen from your office." He left without a word, returning a minute later.

"What are you up to, Peaches?" Milo asked, smiling.

He had always been a handsome kid, Sydney thought. She never would have guessed the stoner freshman who used to toke up under the bleachers while she ran cheerleading practice would turn out to be a beloved brother-in-law. You never knew about some people. They could turn out to have hidden depths of goodness or, as in her case, hidden depths of strength.

"I'm about to show the world what happens when a good Kentucky girl gets riled," she proclaimed.

"Peaches 2.0," Milo said, with a knowing nod to Jessamine.

"It's a sight to behold," Jessamine agreed, smiling up at her sister-in-law. "She's always been something to aspire to, our Peaches."

Sydney tossed her a wink and picked up the tray of cookies they hadn't yet touched, foisting the loaded tray of drinks on Joe. Together they walked outside and handed them out to the reporters camped at the edge of their property. The reporters hurled questions at them, but Peaches deflected them with polite chatter, eventually charming them into curious silence.

"Did everyone get a drink and cookies?" She paused to make sure. "Good. Here, let's all move to the shade. This day is turning out to be a scorcher." They trooped to the shade of a nearby tree. "Would y'all mind sitting down? I usually prefer my husband to be the only man who towers over me." Compliantly, they sat on the grass before her. It was like kindergarten all over again, and she smiled. "Thank you so much. Now, there have been so many questions, and we are so happy to make a statement. Joe's going to pass around a piece of paper, and if you all would be so kind as to fill out your email address, I have something to pass along to you."

A guy in the back raised his hand. "What is it?"

"Oh, well, it's just a little recording of the so-called event in question, the one that clearly shows my husband standing perfectly still while Miss Rodgers advanced and kissed him without permission. And then shows him immediately walking away. I'll also be passing along her work history and the three failed lawsuits she has attempted to bring against former employers for similar incidents. Oh, and maybe, if you're lucky, I'll attach a copy of our counter suit. We're going to be suing her for libel, defamation of character, filing a false report, and taking a severance under false pretenses. I'm certain you can imagine this has been a trying time, what with my husband being falsely accused in such a grievous manner. But feel free to ask any of your questions in a return email, and I'll try to get to them as I have time. Thank y'all so much for your attentive patience. Have a nice day." She linked her arm with Joe's and, together, they walked back to the house, the stunned silence of twenty journalists following in their wake.

CHAPTER 31

The next few weeks were impossibly peaceful. Samantha Rogers dropped her suit, after her lawyer dropped her. She returned her severance. In return, Sydney dropped her countersuit. The media frenzy died down, and she finished prepping the shower that would take place at the end of summer. It was time to start readying her classroom for school's return, but so far she hadn't found the heart to begin. Something felt different this year, and she couldn't put her finger on what it was.

She found, as the combined baby shower drew nearer, that she was looking forward to it more than she would have imagined possible, and not merely because it was fun to throw a party. Ever since her midnight conversation with Joe, after she threw away all her pregnancy tests and put that dream away, she had been feeling an expectant sort of excitement, waiting for the next big thing to come along. She would likely never be a mother to a biological child, but there had to be something else out there for her, a dream bigger than one she could currently imagine. The trick was to find it before she lost heart again.

In the meantime, she would soon become an aunt again, four times over, and being an aunt was pretty great. She glanced at her two oldest nieces, Iz and Justice, currently laughing as they used a helium tank to blow up balloons for the shower.

Justice had arrived on her doorstep the day before, looking squirmy and miserable. "Aunt Syd, can I talk to you?"

"Sure, baby," Sydney replied, opening the door to allow her access.

Justice took a deep breath. "I've been feeling really bad about… about the baby." Her eyes filled with tears.

"Have you talked to anyone about it? I would pay for counseling," Sydney offered.

"It's not that," Justice said, brushing at her eyes. "I know you wanted it, so I wanted you to know if it ever happens again, I want you and Uncle Joe to have it. For real. I won't have an abortion again, I'll give it to you."

It was like being poked with a long, sharp stick, one that stirred up all the old emotions and feelings. Sydney took her own deep breath. "I appreciate that thought, Justice. I really hope the next time you get pregnant you are graduated, educated, employed, and married so you can keep the baby for yourself. But if not, I hope you will choose adoption. And if you do, I hope you will choose a nice, loving family, because there are a lot of good ones out there. But it can't be me. I can't be your unexpected pregnancy backup, well-intentioned as I know you mean it right now. It's too hard for me, the waiting, the hoping, the wanting. I'm taking a dive, taking myself out of the running for my own sanity."

Justice had nodded, weepy, trying to understand impossible adult situations she was in no way prepared to process. Sydney felt so bad she invited her to spend the night and invited Iz, too, deciding to have an impromptu aunt and niece girls' night with face masks, manicures, ice cream and cookies. Sydney always thought she leaned toward small children, precious little buds like her beloved kindergarteners. But teenagers were pretty amazing, too. Maybe the new restlessness was born of desiring to teach a different age. Maybe she should make a lateral move to middle school. Something to ponder.

The baby shower came together without a hitch, even weaving together four different themes for four vastly different women hadn't caused a hiccup.

"It's so lovely," Marie said, giving her a hard squeeze. "You were right about the catering and banquet space. I don't know why I cling so hard to doing it all my way."

"That's because your way is pretty spectacular, and we love it," Sydney assured her, giving her a squeeze in return. "But sometimes you get to take the day off, to be our Mama who relaxes instead of our Mama who works her fingers to the bone taking care of us all."

"It's so pleasant, Peaches. I might start ordering out sometimes," Marie said, clapping her hand over her mouth as if she couldn't believe the words had escaped.

"Marie 2.0," Sydney said.

"Oh, sweetheart, the world's not ready for that," Marie said, scurrying away to greet someone else she knew.

"And when's it going to be your turn, Miss Peaches? You're well overdue for a baby of your own." An acquaintance from church sidled up and asked the dreaded question, for the third time that day.

Sydney assumed her homecoming queen smile. "Never, Miss Boudine, because I'm barren. Try those cucumber sandwiches, they're divine." She tipped her punch to the woman and made a hasty escape, allowing Miss Boudine to do what she would with her mortification. People were well intentioned and merely trying to make conversation, or so Sydney repeatedly told herself. As ever, she brushed the conversation aside and moved on, finding someone else to greet and draw into conversation.

The next morning, when Joe arrived at work, his siblings were waiting for him, faces serious. He stopped short and stared at them, unable to guess the current crisis. "What's up?"

"We need to talk to you," Benny said.

"OK," Joe replied, wariness growing. "Did something else happen with the lawsuit?"

"No, that appears to be over. And our producer assures me Peaches got us the sympathy vote, so it didn't really do anything to affect production. The show will go on, or so they say," Jessamine said.

"Oh, great," Joe replied. He wasn't a fan of the cameras, of parading their lives on TV as entertainment, as if they weren't real people. But everyone else seemed in favor, so he went along and kept his head down for the sake of family unity.

Benny cleared his throat, redirecting attention to him. "The thing is, Joe, you're fired."

Joe blinked at him. "What?"

Giovanni leaned forward and rested his elbows on his knees. "We took a vote, and you're out."

Joe glanced at Moss, with whom he'd always had the deepest big brother to little brother bond. Moss had been his baby as much as his parents'. Moss made a sinister slitting motion across his throat.

"Is this about what happened with Samantha and the lawsuit?" Joe asked.

"Of course not," Jessamine said, waving her hand impatiently.

"I feel like I'm missing something," Joe said.

Benny sighed. "You've done a great job here, really. You've grown the company by leaps and bounds, increased the bottom line. Been a fair and compassionate leader. But we feel your skills would be best served somewhere else."

Joe blinked at him, unable to read his poker face. "What?"

Benny handed him a folder. "This might explain."

Joe took the folder, opened it, and immediately understood. He had to blink a few times to get the moisture out of his eyes before he could speak. "Are you all really okay with this?"

"We took a vote. It was a unanimous Samperi decision," Moss said, voice husky.

"You've given us so much, Joe," Jessamine said. "Let us give this to you."

"It might be the first time Moss and I have ever agreed. Mark it down," Giovanni said.

Joe surveyed their faces and gave up on the pretense of not crying. He swiped at his eyes, but it didn't matter because there were too many tears, not only on his face but on the faces of his brothers and sister, too.

"She's going to love it. And I just love y'all so much," he managed in an imitation of his wife's sweet, southern drawl and leaned in for one, big Samperi hug.

CHAPTER 32

Seventh grade, day two. "Look around, people. This will be your assigned seat for the rest of the semester," their teacher, Mr. Kruger announced. Joe secretly thanked his lucky stars he had sat behind Sydney again. She turned to face him with a smile that made his heart flip. All the girls back home in Brooklyn were similarly Italian, with olive skin and dark hair to match his. Sydney was the first girl he had ever known with pale skin, light blond hair, and green eyes. He got caught up staring at that smile, not realizing at first she had spoken.

"Hey. Looks like we're stuck with each other, Joey." Her head tipped. "Does anyone call you Joey?"

"No, everyone calls me Joe, unless I'm in trouble. Then it's Joseph."

"Maybe I should call you Joey, would that be okay?"

"I guess that would be fine," Joe said, letting his hair flop over his eyes, swallowing hard. Sydney's gaze followed the flop of his hair, staring. His cheeks flushed. Did she think his hair was stupid? The gesture odd? Why was she staring?

"Psst, Samperi." The boy beside him, the one who tried to warn him away from Sydney, now called his name.

"What?" Joe said, turning to face him with a scowl that must have been impressive because the boy flinched.

"I heard your family lives in a barn. Here in Kentucky, that's where our horses live."

Joe didn't react, but inside he crumpled. How did people know they were living in a barn? They were strangers here. Were people talking about them?

Sydney leaned forward. "Hey, Brad, I hear your dad was arrested for growing weed. Again."

"Hey, Sydney, he probably got arrested for selling it to your mom," Brad replied. It might have been an innocuous "your mom" comeback, except for the way Sydney flinched.

"Hey, Brad," Joe said, leaning forward, placing himself protectively in front of Brad's view of Sydney. "Shut up." He didn't actually intend to flex his muscles in a threatening manner, but it must be a thing that happened now that he had them.

Brad sat back with a gesture that let them know the conversation probably wasn't over. Sydney turned back around, facing forward, tips of her ears pink. Joe poked her. "Psst, Peaches."

She faced him, pretty cheeks made prettier by a blush. " Yes, Joey?"

He forgot what he was going to say and had to blink at her a few times to remember. "When did you get so tough?" Yesterday when she had been the target of Brad's ire, she had shrunk into herself, trying to disappear.

She wriggled, pleased by the description. "I don't like people who pick on my friends."

"Is that what we are, friends?"

Her flush deepened. She shrugged and faced forward. He tapped her again. "Psst, Peaches."

She turned back around.

He leaned forward to whisper in her ear. "We actually do live in a barn. It still smells like horses. Want to come see?"

Her eyes lit with an excitement he couldn't possibly discern. Did she actually want to come that badly? She nodded, lips pressed together to try and conceal her smile.

"We live close enough to walk," he added.

She leaned to whisper in return, her breath skirting his ear. "I know where you live, Joey Samperi."

His heart thumped, considering the ramifications of that statement. Had she been watching him? Or did everyone know about the weird new people from Brooklyn? "Ask your mom if you can come home with me tomorrow."

"My mom won't care when I go or how long I stay," she said, her eyes turning so sad he couldn't stand it. She had the type of face that should never be anything but happy.

He crooked his finger to motion her forward, leaning to whisper in her ear again. "Then come home with me tonight. I have to warn you my family is insane." She snickered, and he smiled. "I'm serious. My parents yell and scream everything they say, and I have three little brothers and a sister. They're rotten and wild, all of them." The other day someone in the hardware store had called his siblings hooligans. He had no idea what that meant, but it hadn't sounded good.

She tipped her head, her turn to whisper. "I can't hardly wait."

"Think it through," he said with mock seriousness. "Once you're in, you're one of us for life."

She reached out, resting both hands lightly on his forearm. Joe's heart went into a rhythm that threatened to end him. "Put me in, Joey. I'm ready."

Sydney knew something was amiss when Joe arrived home at noon on a workday. That, plus the fact he'd obviously been crying, screamed that something dire had happened, another crisis loomed on their horizon. She steeled herself, bracing for the worst.

At this point, I can handle anything. Bring it, she thought, tossing back her hair and straightening her shoulders. "What's wrong? What's happened?"

Joe took a breath. "I got fired today."

Her lashes fluttered, sure she had misheard him. "What?"

"Fired. I've been fired."

"You can't be fired. You own the company."

"I own one sixth of the company. My brothers and sister got together and decided they've had enough and I'm done."

"You're speaking gibberish," Sydney said.

"I really wish I were, Peaches, but I'm not kidding. They fired me. Call any one of them and ask." He held out his phone to her. She took it, frowning, not understanding what was happening. His words didn't match his tone or demeanor. Something was off. She flicked his phone awake, intending to call his mother for clues, when he spoke again.

"I think they felt bad about it, of course. And Benny, being the good guy he is, found another job."

"Another construction company?" she tried. Were they branching out? Buying another company? Was Joe about to double his workload?

"Oh, no, baby, I'm not qualified for this job."

"Joey, I don't have the patience of a lovestruck twelve year old anymore. Could you find a point, please?"

"There was a job opening. Benny was on the search committee, and he took the liberty of putting in a resume."

"He put in your resume without asking?"

"No, baby, he put in your resume without asking." He handed her a folder. She opened it and began to read.

"Foundations Orphanage, Entebbe, Uganda." She glanced up at him, confused, but heart beating hard with anticipation regardless. "What is this place?"

"It's an all girls orphanage in Uganda. They're looking for a new director, someone to live on site, care for 33 girls, from birth to sixteen. They need someone to educate them, train and mentor them, love them. Kind of like a mom."

She opened her mouth, but no sound came out.

"And of course they'll need a dad." He pointed to his chest.

"Is this for real?" she whispered, dashing at her eyes.

He nodded, dashing at his eyes, too. "What do you say, Peaches? You ready for a whole, new grand adventure, a different kind of magic?"

"I say *hey*." She tumbled into his arms, laughing and crying. They jumped up and down, spinning in a circle, around and around their kitchen.

"Joe and Peaches 2.0," he whispered.

"Joe and Peaches 2.0 forever and ever," she agreed.

"Amen," Joe said and kissed her.

. . .

Thank you for reading this book, as well as all the Builders Series. For more books, please visit my website at www.vanessagraybartal.com

www.ingramcontent.com/pod-product-compliance
Lightning Source LLC
Chambersburg PA
CBHW030640190726
48286CB00008B/2601